GOD said...

"Let there be love"

Albert Davidoo & George G. Edwards

God said... "Let There Be Love"

First published 2013

Published by: Davidoo & Edwards Publishing

16055 Ventura Blvd. #1225
Encino, CA, 91436
Email: davidoocpa@aol.com
George.edwards1977@gmail.com

Phone: 818-501-8866 Fax: 818-501-8931

URL: godsaidlettherebelove.com

Original illustrations by Renee Barratt
Printed by Ingram
God said... "Let There Be Love"
Davidoo, Albert; Edwards, George G.
ISBN 978-0-9910288-0-1

Table of Contents

Introduction

Albert Davidoo & George G. Edwards bring to life this captivating tale inspired by a true story. Follow along as this journey of faith, the pendulum we call life, and the quintessential meaning of unconditional love sends you on a most passionate array of emotions. Sharing the belief that love and compassion can unite the world, this story embodies their message.

Prologue

A painful ringing pierced my ears. Gravel and darkness surrounded me. A warm and sunny day, which began with such promise, had now crossed into something directly out of a horror film. Voices began whispering cries of anguish and terror. I tried moving around, but to no avail – I was trapped in this nightmare.

I must be dazed or dreaming, I thought to myself, which was the reason I couldn't climb to my feet. If not, then what? I tried standing, but landed face first on the road again. Only this time, I felt hopelessly glued to the ground. I extended my neck high enough to witness the macabre scene of terror that lay before me.

Sounds of agony surrounded me, holding me hostage. A few, seemingly terrified, individuals were scrambling in front of me. Yet I remained abandoned, awaiting relief of any kind. I watched children being carried to safety, while others assisted the elderly and women who were hurt as well.

I soon recognized strangers in the crowd, thinking to myself, I'm foreign no more. I struggled to get their attention as they moved directly past me. Some ran by without a glance my way, like I was invisible. I could see our priest amongst the chaotic crowd, drenched in blood, being assisted by other men who were also aiding those scattered across the ground.

I looked on in horror at the blood and flesh strewn along the road, the stench of burnt human remains seared my senses. I tried in vain to call out for help again, but I was ignored, the townsmen continued on without me. I was terrified and helpless. I couldn't stand on my feet no matter how hard I battled.

I slowly faded away in comfort, I grew numb, and my senses dulled. The smell that haunted me only seconds earlier had been erased with emptiness. I laid my face down on the concrete in submission, while staring sideways at the feet running by me. I noticed more grizzly scenes of torn flesh and splattered blood along the road.

A striking flash of light caught my eye. I tried focusing on the object responsible for the brief flicker of hope. Finally, I realized what was causing this momentary flare. The cross that stood atop the church this morning had now been cast down from above – into the hell that waited below.

Lying sideways, the crucifix caught what was left of the sun, causing it to shine directly at me. I grew hypnotized by the ray of light, almost consoled.

I stared at this object for what seemed like an eternity, before feeling a rush of anxiety growing inside me. My existence began shrinking with each passing moment. The darkness slowly crept in, surrounding me as I struggled to move. Suddenly, it hit me. Could it really be... am I dead?

Chapter 1

*T*he story of my life has been both unique and rewarding to say the least. Being a Christian, born in an Islamic country, has a nature all its own. The events in my life have shaped me into a more resilient and faithful man. I am able to appreciate my history, a past that includes moments of agony and misery that I will soon share with you. My life journey has consisted of struggles that enabled me to define myself and even more, to appreciate the true value of life.

Although, today, I live by the motto that *I must try to leave this planet in a better condition than when I arrived,* there have been many folks who have influenced my journey – each possessing a unique gift to share with the world. They taught me to view myself spiritually, rather than what is visible to the naked eye. Leading me to this epiphany – true happiness comes from within.

I was born on a cold and snowy December night in 1990, near the Shaqlawa providence, in Northern Iraq. I was delivered only eighteen minutes earlier than my twin brother. Yet, as you will soon discover, those few moments have changed my life forever.

My dear mother, Miriam, welcomed us into the world with the help of midwives, from our home. This was a common practice in those days for most women in my village. What made our labor more difficult than other pregnancies was the fact that I was a twin. A child, along with his mother, did not achieve the survival rates we enjoy today. So delivering twins only compounded the risks, reducing our chance of survival.

While I am a healthy fifty-two years old today, many times in my life, I never believed I'd reach this age. Though I must admit, I am pleasantly surprised to have made it this far. This was a pattern in which my life would follow. Nothing was going to come easy to me, and my birth was proof.

I was given the name Paul, while my twin brother was named Robert. Following a family tradition, my brother and I were given the names of our grandfathers - from both sides of the family.

During the first few months of my life, my inexperienced mother required help from her sisters. My aunts assisted with changing our clothes, preparing food, and even giving us our regular baths.

In addition to the daily routine, my aunts carried out the more exhausting responsibilities of staying up with us those many sleepless nights when we were ill. A year after the birth of twins, my mother was blessed with her third son, my youngest brother, Peter.

He was named after Peter from the Bible, which meant *Rock,* derived from the Greek language. My father believed a child's name was more than just a tag that could influence the chosen path in life – it was a title.

In our tradition, having a boy was symbolic. Add the fact that I was one half of twin boys, only made it twice as special. You see, in our culture, having boys meant that the parents would be able to pass on the family name, traditions, and responsibilities. Our lineage would continue on, at least another generation – and hopefully more.

My father, being an only son, understood the significance of having multiple boys. He was the sole provider of our family, taking good care of my grand-parents who also lived with us, and hoped we'd return the favor when my brothers and I reached adulthood.

"Paul, go outside and cut up some more lumber for the fireplace," My father, Daniel, ordered from the living room.

"Can you please ask Peter or Robert to chop wood today?" I replied. Frustrated with the long list of chores I completed daily.

"No, I asked you. Now get out there and do as you're told," losing his temper, he shouted. Something my father was known to do.

Although only by a few minutes, being the oldest of my siblings, I was the leader by birth. And as the eldest, I was *unofficially* responsible for my brothers.

Unfortunately, it also meant I would carry the majority of the household tasks as well.

Nevertheless, I always tried to encourage my brothers to do their best in anything they attempted. The mutual feeling of respect we shared continued for many years. However, with time, we slowly began to develop our own identities.

Over the years, it became my unspoken duty, an obligation if you will, to be my brothers' keeper. I welcomed the responsibility of taking them under my wing, for it was my commitment. Even today, I remain a mentor, a source of strength, to my family. Due to this tradition, along with the sacrifices I have made, a special character was created. Ultimately, shaping me into the man I am today.

Looking back on my life, I believe God had a special mission for me. As I soon discovered, before any happiness was to be realized, my life would first hit rock-bottom.

Chapter 2

I grew up in a small Northern Iraq village. My family spent their entire lives in this part of the region. My forefathers, the Assyrians, along with their cousins, the Babylonians, were the natives of this land. We have preserved our inherent Aramaic tongue throughout the years, despite living in a predominantly Arab land over the last six centuries or so.

Living in a small neighborhood had both its benefits and shortcomings, as does any tiny city. In our community, we did not have medical centers or clinics readily available. In lieu of the luxury that big city hospitals and their treatment afforded, we depended, almost exclusively, on our village locals. Each neighbor specialized in one area of our lives. Together, we forged a self-sufficient society.

"Good afternoon, Daniel," our doctor, Ashur, declared to my father in passing.

"Good afternoon to you, Doctor. How is everyone doing today?" my father replied, although never visiting a doctor in his life himself.

"Everyone is fine, thank God," Dr. Ashur replied.

It's funny to see a doctor giving credit to an invisible deity, instead of the advancements enjoyed in the medical field. Nevertheless, in those days and in that town, it was a common scene.

Resident medics visited the village homes weekly to ensure that everyone was doing well. The physician carried a medicine bag from home to home, performing his magic for all those in need of a cure. Although some locals concocted their own natural remedies made from herbs and spices to cure their illness, doctor visits remained the norm.

My grandfather built our house with his hands almost fifty years ago. He constructed it on a foundation comprised of two essential principles, family and love. There was a lifetime of history residing within the walls of that simple three bedroom house, in a village that most people have never heard of.

My town consisted of approximately fifteen hundred residents. All of our citizens were essentially one big family. A few neighbors raised chickens, while others tended to the sheep, and some housed the cows for milk. We were a tightknit community, like any small village, which relied on its own resources for daily needs.

I was living on historic and sacred land, which might

explain the unique events in my life. The spirits of my ancestors, the mighty sons of the Sumerians, shared these same ancient grounds. Or maybe my eighty-one-year-old grandmother was correct when she'd tease us by saying; *something is in the water, making everyone a bit crazy* – I bought into her conspiracy as well.

During the 1990s, Iraq's Christian citizens were estimated at more than one million, with the largest concentration occupying Northern Iraq. Better known today as, the Kurdistan Region.

However, after the Gulf War in 1991, my community collapsed into a state of confusion and panic. My people, who were now the minority, feared for their lives after encountering religious violence and prejudice.

As if living under the iron fist of Saddam Hussein, infamously known as the Butcher of Baghdad, for all those years, wasn't punishment enough. Premeditated attacks against our churches and homes, with planted explosives, became routine.

Our families lived with the daily threat of being assaulted by radical Muslim militants. Radicals, who intentionally targeted our community with physical violence, also used rape as an instrument of terror against our women.

These extremists planted explosives in the basements of churches, homes, and sometimes even elementary schools. Many families were uprooted, forced to flee a land they had called home since the dawn of time. Natives seeking refuge, and relief, abandoned the country that was once their only identity.

Miles away from the explosions that lit up the skies of the city, our small town of Shaqlawa emerged as a sanctuary. Many families pursuing peace over the violence that haunted their day-to-day lives resided there. Not too far north of us, under Kurdish control, Mergasur Province became the passageway for those looking to flee the religious bigotry that plagued our country.

Adjacent to Shaqlawa was a town called Erbil. The small village, from a distance, resembled any other city in the northern regions of Iraq. Still, if you ever spend some time there, you'd recognize the *American* influences adopted by our youth. Religious obedience was slowly replaced with modern progress and lofty ambitions.

"I will travel the world one day," I proclaimed, my friends now laughing at my ambition.

"Sure, if by world, you mean Iraq," William, a childhood friend of mine, replied sarcastically.

"Watch and see, William, I will send you postcards from all four corners of the earth," I replied, smiling and sipping on a cold soda.

"That will be difficult to accomplish, considering the earth is round," William said, while snickering at my comment.

William joked again, "Do me a favor and just send me pictures of women from European countries, or from America," he continued laughing, as he jabbed me in the shoulder with his fist.

My friends and I fantasized about living the American Dream, or the Hollywood version of it. While the vast majority only thought about surviving, never mind living a fairytale. Though with each passing day we remained in this diverse land, seemingly trapped in the Middle-Ages, the more our window of opportunity withered.

While growing up, I was plagued with nightmares as far as I can remember. My mother told me about an incident that happened to me when I was about five or six years old. I dreamt that my uncle lost his teeth in an automobile accident. Two weeks later, though not in a car wreck, my uncle unexpectedly died.

At thirteen years of age, I began having these visions again. Though now they started with me under my bed covers. However, this last dream, I wasn't alone. To my surprise, I found myself with a stranger. She and I were tucked under my covers, hiding from our parents, eating cookies instead of sleeping. Yet each time she offered me a cookie, my two front teeth fell out. Blood would cascade from my mouth and onto the floor.

I'd wake up in a pool of sweat, sometimes in tears, barely catching my breath. I was terrified about my visions, largely in part because I believed in the superstition that losing teeth, in a dream, meant some terrible accident was to follow.

I didn't tell my parents about my nightmares any longer. I was afraid of its implications, denying what I felt in my gut. My chance at a happy life in America was becoming a long shot with each passing moment.

I was frightened of this omen. Yet I kept quiet, continuing my daily routine as if nothing was bothering me. However, in my mind, I was in a race with time – a duel, not many have won.

Chapter 3

O ne of the most cherished traditions my family passed on from one generation to the next, was our family dinners together. After we finished supper, we enjoyed a sweet dessert. However, due to their scarce availability, treats were a rare pleasure. My personal favorite was Baklava with chai, of course, made from my grandmother's special ingredients.

If we behaved, we also enjoyed a night of storytelling that involved action and adventure. Since each tale contained a moral lesson to be learned, my grandpa, Sargon, would set the grandkids down to discover what, if anything, we've learned.

He began by reading passages from the Bible, which were written in Aramaic. After reading selected verses, he allowed us to share our thoughts on each passage and what it meant to us personally. Despite being only thirteen at the time, I remember an evening when I was so eager to skip dinner, and have dessert, that I foolishly requested my grandfather to rush our lesson.

"Can we pick a short verse from the Bible grandpa," I asked, without thinking of the consequences.

He immediately turned towards me with a look that would have melted the cold winter ice.

"Maybe you'd like to go to bed without dessert tonight?" My grandfather replied, sarcastically, yet retaining that smile that we adored.

"Sorry grandpa, I love your stories. I just wanted to ..." I attempted to repair that damage I had done just a few moments earlier.

He smiled at me and ruffled my hair. "Don't worry, at your age, I couldn't sit still either."

Nonetheless, I was so captivated by what he shared, that I'd remain daydreaming about it long after he dismissed us. Sometimes forgetting all about the dessert I craved so desperately earlier.

The passage he recited to us was from the book of Matthew, verse 25:35-37; *for I was hungry and you gave me food; I was thirsty and you gave me drink; I was a stranger and you took me in. I was naked and you clothed me; I was sick and you visited me; I was in prison and you came to me; then the righteous will answer him, saying, "Lord, when did we see you hungry and feed you, or thirsty and gave you drink?*

My granddad paused, "Are you boys following along?"

he asked, as his eyes combed over my brothers and I.

He continued reading aloud, *"And when did we see you a stranger and take you in, or naked and clothe you?' or when did we see you sick, or in prison, and come to you? And the King will answer and say to them, 'Assuredly, I say to you, in as much as you did it to one of the least of these my brethren, you did it to me."*

Robert and Peter both tried to answer the question. But I knew this was meant more for me, because of my role as the eldest, of course. Later in my life, I would come to understand, and truly appreciate, the lesson hidden within the passage.

I recognized and accepted my duty as guardian to my brothers and family. Protecting them from any harm that may come their way was my responsibility. These passages, my grandpa read to us as children, remained the foundation in which I have handled all the trials and tribulations in my life.

My grandpa also taught us our native alphabet, including a few Arabic words. Although he was born in a predominantly Arab speaking country, he never truly admitted to knowing the language well. He was a noble man, my grandpa. He was extremely proud of his heritage, and stubborn in his stance, the only language he needed to pass on was his own.

He also instilled the principle of *fear no man*, and no punishment inflicted, for that matter. Though, he did make it clear that we should abide by the laws of the land, if it did not conflict with our integrity, or the teachings of the Bible. His view and passion for his principles and tradition could not be compromised. My grandpa was a man of integrity, honesty, and honor above all.

"You stand up for your rights, no matter what the consequence might be," grandpa Sargon said, sternly.

My brothers and I sat in silence for a moment, not sure what to say, "What if they threaten to kill us?" I timidly replied.

"We're all going to die!" he immediately answered, his voice now full of vigor, "It is important that you live with honor and your integrity intact," he added, violently waving his finger in the air.

Religion couldn't be the only reason my family feuded with Arabs, I thought to myself.

"Why do you hate Muslims grandpa?" I asked, wanting to understand why such resentment towards an entire group of people.

"I don't hate Muslims Paul, I love my people. Do you understand the difference?" my grandfather asked.

"No. Not really," Peter chimed in.

"Members of our family, our community, have been murdered in multiple genocides by Muslims since Islam was founded," He said, with watery eyes, but a stern voice.

I thought my grandfather was extreme in his beliefs, even a bit outdated, especially on topics such as religion. I feared he unconsciously adopted the dangerous behavior of radical Muslims he despised. I didn't believe all Muslims were terrorists, like not all Christians follow the Bible word-for-word.

I still didn't quite understand why my grandpa, and family for that matter, despised the vast majority of Muslims. Nonetheless, the universe seems to have a mind of its own, and soon, I'd hear from it.

Chapter 4

Although I finally accepted the fact that my grandpa was a bit extreme, I understood that the village elders were all similar in their philosophy. The way in which he handled himself was universally accepted as the norm in my community, and all men were to carry on this moral code. The townsmen lived their lives, just as the martyrs before them did, to protect their cultural identity.

That was fine by me though, because it allowed my brothers and me to create an unbreakable oath. I formed an inseparable bond with them, we were a team.

We recognized that working together would tilt the odds in our favor against any challenge, or confrontation, we faced growing up. We learned early on, and promised, to keep it that way no matter how many years would pass.

"We kicked their butts all over the field!" Peter shouted, pumping his fist in the air.

I placed both my hands on my brother's shoulders, "Listen to me, if we stick together, nobody will beat us at anything," I said, to both Peter and Robert.

"We will always be together, right?" Robert asked, looking directly at me.

"Of course, I will never abandon any of you. Where ever I go, I will take you both with me," I said, while tousling Peter's shoulder length hair that he was so fond of.

While modest in technologically, our village was magnificent in its scenery. It was situated amid three mountains, resting in the middle of flowing creeks and age old trees.

We enjoyed blissful weather more than most regions and rarely were we forced to endure one-sided climate conditions. A charming spring was followed by a sizzling summer, subtly embracing the fresh autumn wind, while finally settling on a tranquil, and picturesque, winter.

When not in school, we often played soccer after we had breakfast. Occasionally taking naps in the afternoons, while closing out the night by fishing into the late hours. In those warmer months, villagers would wash their garments in the creek near my home. My family did our spring cleaning in the summer as well.

The wives and daughters were responsible for taking care of the cooking, cleaning, and laundry. The men reinforced the house, preparing for the upcoming autumn rain and winter snow.

Each fall, our grandmothers sewed us handcrafted sweaters, preparing us for the unforgiving winter that sometimes invaded our village. While logs and canned food were preserved in our shed.

As the months turned colder, we spent countless hours with our parents. That provided us the opportunity to learn more about our history, our family, and our nation. I do recall though, just how fond we were of the radio.

When any type of broadcast played western music, my family gathered around and listened for hours, truly the highlight of our day. The following morning, kids in my village talked about what they heard the night prior. We tested one another on who memorized most of the lyrics. I typically fared better than the rest, largely crediting my attention to detail.

"Plenty of time at the hotel..." William sang, or at least attempted to sing.

"What was that?" I sarcastically asked.

"Big Hotel California," William replied, laughing with the other guys.

"Welcome to the Hotel California, such a lovely place, such a lovely face. Plenty of room at the Hotel California," I continued singing the chorus line, while also humming the words I hadn't quite memorized yet.

"What band sings that song?" I quizzed my friends.

"The hawks or crows, I think. Some type of bird," William guessed, though I believe he was mocking me.

"The eagles, you clown," I playfully replied, as he so often does.

Although we had plenty of resources to sustain us through the Christmas season, during the winter, our diet changed. We relied strictly on what the land provided as our source of nutrition.

During those brief cold winter months, meat was almost absent from our supply. Instead, eggs would become a valuable and alternative source of protein. We would trade resources such as milk and bread, for stamps and writing paper, with neighboring villages.

I even taught myself to read and write Arabic. I earned a few coins translating our neighbor's mail, and helped around the community. Many of the elders were illiterate, allowing my education to come in handy.

While the few extra few dollars were helpful at the time, my education was something I would invest in for the rest of my life.

Consequently, as with any town lacking in a particular area, someone had to step up and fill the void. With very few of neighbors having any type of education, positions requiring any type of schooling become a high demand.

Unfortunately, when only a handful of individuals in town are literate – greed, betrayal, and chaos is sure to follow.

Chapter 5

*T*he foundation of our village was a tiny old church in the heart of our neighborhood. Every Sunday, our people gathered to hear Father George deliver his sermon. It was the essence of our existence, the focus of all our lives. I remember enjoying the time I spent with family, no matter where we were.

I looked forward to mass on Sunday more than usual as I grew older, largely due to the fact that I'd be able to see my neighbor. She was a beautiful and feisty young girl named Ishtar. This beauty was the love of my life, and soon, she'd change my entire existence.

Grandpa Sargon always got us ready for church on Sunday, and led the way. Shaqlawa only had one church, and it was widely accepted as the pillar of our community.

Father George would sleep in the cottage located at the back of the church. He was, without a doubt, a wise and moral man. Proud, and strong, like the rest of the men in my village.

Although the church backyard was small, it was often used to host special occasions. This allowed neighbors to gather around catching up on events, sing songs, drink, or just simply enjoy each other's company.

The women in our family typically gathered in a separate room, and gossip was the topic of the conversation – though it wasn't admitted. While the men gathered around a fire laughing, playing backgammon, and discussing politics.

I was always curious about the subjects the adult's discussed, but never was allowed to listen in because of my age. However, when I was twelve years old, I tried to impress my brothers by participating in conversations typically reserved for the grown-ups.

"What are you doing here Paul?" my father asked, while the other men stood around waiting for my answer.

I froze for a moment, "Nothing, just listening to the conversation," I barely managed to say, looking up at them now, hoping the storm had passed.

He replied with a chuckle, "Get lost. Go find your brothers or friends. This is not for kids, now beat it."

Despite being rejected, I wasn't discouraged. In fact, I knew that I'd made an impression with the adults. I wasn't just a kid. I was a man - almost.

The highlights of our village were times when

relatives, who resided outside of our country, would visit. Pretty girls, dressed in exquisite European fashion, would stay for a month or so. Although mainly speaking Aramaic, and some Arabic, they occasionally used *Western lingo* to impress us.

Contrary to the dark haired girls in our village, these women dyed their hairs blonde, with streaks of different colors as well. Our eccentric visitors had no trouble making new friends with the youth. They constantly spoke about their fascinating lives around the world, yet it was one particular country that captivated me – The United States of America.

"What's it like in America?" I asked my cousin, who currently lived in the United States.

She smiled and replied, "Close your eyes... now picture anything you can possibly desire," leaving me to my wild, and creative, imagination,

"Anything?" I asked to confirm.

"Yes," she nodded.

I spent the next few days' fantasizing about the unlimited opportunities that awaited me, outside my city.

"Mom, I want to move the United States when I am older," I said, waiting for her reaction.

"America, huh?" she replied, slightly bobbing her head back and forth, in thought.

"Yes, no matter what it takes. I don't care if I live in the streets. I will live my dream," I continued, staring off into the sky from the kitchen window.

"Let's see how well you do here first, before you try to

become the next Elvis Presley," she said, flashing her loving smile.

We stood together in silence, daydreaming.

She glanced back at me, "What is wrong with your homeland?" stopping her chores in anticipation of an immediate response.

"Nothing," I mumbled, "Just thought..."

"Remember, Paul, it is the quality of life that is important, not the quantity," she interrupted, looking down into the sink.

I left the kitchen contemplating just how bad I wanted to move to the United States. It was something I desired. Besides, who didn't want to live the *American Dream*?

Although I loved my homeland, I wanted more than what was available, I dreamt big! Don't get me wrong, living in a tight-knit community had its perks.

However, like in every village, town, or city, there were a few bad apples - a darker side. Villains, so to speak, and our tiny land was no exception. Rumors and secrets, hidden in plain view, were now boiling over – soon to erupt.

Chapter 6

*O*nly a few houses down from our home lived a neighbor, Abraham, who had two daughters. The older of the two was Ishtar, who I was completely enamored with. The *Goddess of love*, that's what her name meant in our language, and oh how fitting that definition truly was.

I wasn't allowed any contact with her because of the conflict between our fathers. It all started a year earlier when my dad was in charge of handling the church's financial matters. Abraham accused my father of misappropriating church funds, essentially, stealing from the church.

Abraham was a tall and imposing man. His dark hair equaled by his black eyes, and only surpassed by his gloomy soul. He bore a prominent scar over his right eyebrow from a fight, years earlier. Abraham was extremely obnoxious and arrogant. Add ignorant to the mix and you have a recipe for disaster.

Several fights, and screaming matches, ensued between the two stubborn men. One of the confrontations escalated to such a degree, that my father actually spit at Abraham. To many, spitting at another human being is an insult that is unrivaled. It was that incident that pushed our fathers passed the point of no return. Though being small in stature, especially compared to Abraham, my dad was fearless.

An investigation was ordered, and conducted, into the handling of the church funds. The church board assigned to handle the inquiry concluded that my father had committed no illegal acts of any kind.

In light of the ruling, Abraham made several attempts to apologize to my dad. However, being the proud and stubborn man my father was, he refused to forgive or forget.

My people believe that a man's reputation is all one has in life. Abraham damaged my father's honor with what was, in his mind, false accusations. My dad always carried himself with honor, a moral man. However, he wasn't going to let the grudge he held fade that quickly.

One weekend, while my father and grandpa were out of town buying supplies, I found myself with seniority at home, the man of the house. Of course with my luck, my mother came down with a fever of 101°.

My father and Abraham never got along, and maybe never would, but my mother had a terrible fever, and our local doctor was unavailable to help her. Trying not to panic, I ran to our neighbor's house hoping Abraham would not answer the door or turn me away. The hatred that resided within me, towards Abraham, was cast aside – for now.

Abraham's daughters were around my brothers and my age. Ishtar was sixteen, and Mary was four years younger. I hoped that one of the sisters, or possibly their mother, Helen, would answer the door – and my wishes as well.

I knocked on the door a few times and anxiously waited. A million thoughts raced frantically through my mind while I stood at the door.

My lucky day, I thought to myself, as Ishtar answered the door. She greeted me with those beautiful hazel eyes, and a smile that can melt the December snow from the mountain tops. Her hair, layered passed her shoulders, black as the night. Her skin was as smooth as silk - like a porcelain doll. I stared at her for a second, forgetting why I was there. I was mesmerized by her beauty, and my heart was in her hands from that moment on.

"Hi Paul, do you want to come in?" she asked.

I paused to take in the moment, "Yes. I mean, no. My mom is sick. Can you ..."

"Come in, I'll call my mother," she replied, turning towards the living room. Ishtar immediately notified her mother, Helen. Luckily for me, Abraham was not home at the time.

Helen quickly came running, "Where is Miriam?" she asked, rhetorically I presumed. Because, before I could reply, she bolted passed me and towards my house. I tried to tell Helen about my mother's condition, while simultaneously rushing to her aid.

Helen stayed with my mother, nurturing her back to health. Despite our fathers' bitter rivalry, our mothers would remain friends for the rest of their lives.

Following that incident, Ishtar and I rarely spoke for some time. Yet her smile, and face, rested gently in my thoughts. Our eyes met on many occasions, but I couldn't gather the courage to actually talk to her in public. The further I was forbidden to see her, the more a fixture in my dreams she became – both day and night.

After a few months of working up the nerve, I finally gave into the summer's plea. The wind of inspiration carried me along, encouraging me to somehow express my feelings to the love of my life. I contemplated writing her a note and passing it to her myself. However, that option seemed too risky.

I decided to use her younger sister, Mary, as our bridge to one another. I remained a bit apprehensive at first. I feared the possibility she'd turn over the letter to her father, wedging our families further apart, and seal our fate.

I finally wrote the letter and began searching for Mary in our village. To my surprise, I spotted her less than an hour into my quest. She was with a couple of her girlfriends. They were playing together in our neighborhood park.

"Hi Mary," I said, as her friends gathered around us.

She smiled. "Hello Paul. Where is Peter?" she asked,

while trying to conceal her crush on my younger brother.

"He's with Robert, at home. Where is your sister?" I nervously asked.

"Why? Do you like my sister? She's at home. Do you want to visit her?" she quickly, and naively, asked. Maybe she was rubbing in my face the fact that I could not be caught in public with her sister, not yet at least.

I looked around to ensure no adults were watching. "I would love to come over. But you know I can't," I disappointedly replied.

We continued staring at each other for a moment before being interrupted.

"Are we still going to play, or should I go home, Mary?" asked one of her friends, who had now joined our conversation.

Mary and I turned toward her friend with an irritated look on both our faces. She got the message and stayed quiet.

"Well, what is it Paul?" Mary asked. Her patience seemed to be waning with each passing moment of silence.

My thoughts danced on the tip of my tongue. Yet there I was, frozen.

"I have something I want you to give to Ishtar," the mere sound of her name melted my heart and soothed my soul.

She stuck her hand out and nodded. "What does it say?" she said, with a mischievous smile on her face.

"None of your business Mary," I snapped, "You're too

young to read this type of talk."

She pulled her hand back, "Fine, if you don't tell me what's inside that letter, I won't deliver it to my sister," she was blackmailing me before I had committed any crime – just my luck.

"Okay, okay. I'll tell you what's inside. I cannot open it now, because it is sealed," I answered, shaking my head, as her smile grew wider, "However, since you insist, I do know most of the letter by heart."

If Mary decided to read the letter I wrote, proclaiming my love for her sister, I would essentially be at her mercy. However, this way we'd form a bond, build a trust, as friends.

I pulled Mary farther aside. "I love your sister. I want to marry her. I ..."

"How do you know my sister feels the same about you, Paul?" she asked, yet her tone seemed sincere.

I never entertained that possibility, not until now, I realized, "I need to know. I cannot live my life not knowing," I begged.

"I don't know if I want to get involved, Paul," she said, now avoiding eye contact.

I leaned down a bit to catch her eyes, "I love her, she loves me. We will have children together. I will teach my son to play soccer, like his dad," I rambled, as she giggled.

She stuck out her hand, once again, "Give me the letter. I will take it to her. But, you promise to tell Peter I said hi," Mary said, as she blushed and looked away.

I patted her head, "Yes, I will tell him you said hello, Mary," I replied smiling.

To my surprise, she was supportive and quite excited about the possibilities, or at least it seemed that way to me. Mary gladly agreed, promising to make sure her sister received the letter immediately.

I didn't invest too much hope in any type of response in fear of rejection. Though I was confident, I wasn't sure how Ishtar actually felt about me. After all, this obsession was something only I was a part of at this point.

Yet as fate had planned, I received a letter back from Ishtar the next day. Mary delivered the message with a smile. Her optimism shined hope that meant my prayers had been answered.

"Hi Mary," I said, almost whispering, while looking around.

"I've got something for you Paul," she replied, teasingly extending her hand out before pulling the letter back.

After a few playful attempts to snatch the letter from her hands, I stopped and sighed. She continued to smile at me, almost giggling, before finally handing it over.

"Thank you," I managed, barely keeping my composure, "I mean it, Mary, thank you. If there is anything you ever need, or if someone ever bothers you, come to me," I added, knowing this girl would someday be my sister in-law.

Mary smiled and gave me a big hug, "I am happy for the both of you. Now tell me what Peter said about me!"

she continued, her eyes now squinted, pretending to be focused.

"Get out of here. You're too young for love," I said, ruffling her hair.

With a frown now replacing her smile, she added, "Hey, love knows no time, or race, and no religion for that matter...love is blind."

"Yes it is, now run along," I said, watching her skip down the road and towards the park.

I quickly opened the letter and began reading. In the note, Ishtar expressed her feelings were mutual. That she liked me and wanted kids, three to be exact. She also professed having a crush on me for more than a year now. However, she was fearful her father ever caught wind of our love and put an end to it before it began. She went on by saying that this was *our fate* – destiny manifest.

With the anxiety of being caught, still hovering above our heads, Ishtar and I were unable to be seen together. We spent the next few months writing back and forth to each other. It was the most beautiful summer of my young life.

During my *summer of love*, I would join the local boys from my village, out in the fields, to play sports or just cause mischief. I often noticed Ishtar playing with her friends in the distance.

On occasion, I'd catch her smiling at me while I played with friends. The other boys noticed Ishtar as well, making me extremely jealous. When my friends made any comments about her, I found myself in a fit of rage.

"Who are you looking at?" I said to one of the boys playing soccer with us. I used my deepest and most intimidating tone. Standing not more than an inch from his face, I repeated myself.

"Who are you staring at?" I continued. My fists now clenched as tight as my jaw. I was prepared to fight for my future wife.

"Nobody, relax," he replied, backing away a bit.

"Good, because she is off limits," I ordered, my adrenaline now subsiding a bit.

I wasn't a big guy, but I fought like one. I was tough and relentless. That was my greatest strength, my determination to overcome adversity. It proved to be an attribute I'd rely on throughout my life.

Our desire to spend time together had now grown into an unyielding thirst that could only be quenched by our love. Ishtar and I found any excuse to see each other. Religion would now play a vital role in our love life as well.

We hoped both our families would not invest too much time searching for us, or wonder why we were away for so long, especially during mass. With Easter Sunday fast approaching, we knew this would be the opportune time to be together. Ishtar and I selected a secret rendezvous spot we agreed to meet during our *private escapade*.

We had agreed to meet under a tree, located about a mile outside the church, in an open field. This tree was known as the tree of love to the older teens, because it was shaped like a heart. The legend was that those lucky enough to kiss under this tree were to be blessed with a lifetime of happiness.

I felt unusually anxious about ditching mass to meet with a girl. Though I couldn't put my finger on it at first, I knew this meeting would change my life – for better or worse was yet to be determined.

Yet I reminded myself, I was willing to risk my life for her. Unfortunately, I wasn't informed on how much *true love* actually cost. But like everything else in my life, I'd first enroll in a crash course.

Chapter 7

*E*aster was a truly special time for our family, and the entire village for that matter. While my parents prepared for mass, my brothers and I were asked to help with the festivities as well. Our assignment was boiling more than three dozen eggs. We planned on playing a game that was decided by whose egg remained intact.

Though I was given many more chores to finish that weekend, I met with Ishtar to talk about coming out to our families regarding the love we shared.

"I don't think it's a good idea, Paul," she said, while drawing imaginary circles on my palm.

"Why not?" I asked, hoping I'd convince her otherwise.

"My family, my father in particular, would kill me. I

don't mean he'd be just angry at me. He would actually kill me," she replied, shaking her head to emphasize the magnitude of my request.

Ishtar was obviously not too keen on the idea, or at least not as optimistic as I was. But then again, she wasn't a teenage boy.

Having an intimate relationship while not married was frowned upon in my culture, not to mention the shame a girl would bring on her family name as a result. As ridiculous a view it seems in today's society, it was the way of the culture where we were raised.

I thought Easter would be as good a time as any to open the topic of Ishtar and my feelings with our families. Being that it was a special time for our people, I was convinced that the spirit of love, which was in the air, would conquer all doubts.

"You don't think the festive mood will make it easier to announce?" I continued pressing her, hoping she'd break.

"I don't want to disappoint my father, Paul," she said, running her finger across my cheek.

"Disappoint him how?" I asked, confused and offended.

"You know what I mean Paul, it's our culture," she snapped. The mood, now dampened, was shifting from optimism to pessimism in a hurry.

"Let's drop the subject for now. We will cross that bridge when we get there," I said, hoping to pacify the situation.

On Easter Sunday, our families were going to be attending church as planned. I barely slept an hour the night before mass. All that occupied my mind was Ishtar - the love of my life.

"Are you boys up?" I heard my mom shout from the hallway.

"Yes, we're getting dressed," Peter yelled back.

"Are you excited?" Robert asked, staring at me with his infamous smirk.

"What do I have to be excited about?" I replied, pretending not to know what he meant.

"You know what I'm talking about, Paul," He continued smirking, "Ishtar...the Goddess of Love."

"I am a bit anxious, but happy," I replied, "You cannot tell mom about any of this, you understand?" I insisted.

"What about dad?" Peter chimed in, sarcastically.

I clinched my fist in a mock threat, "I'd give you a whipping," I answered, while smiling.

"We don't want to be late to mass. Get your asses downstairs now!" my father yelled. I guess today was not a good day to break the news about my affair, I thought to myself.

We heard mom scolding our father for cursing on a religious holiday, "Daniel, is that really necessary?" she said, sounding annoyed.

"We're coming down!" I shouted back.

I remained quiet the entire trip to mass. I was consumed by one thought - my destiny awaits me. We pulled into the church parking lot just before nine o'clock.

The sun was warm to the skin, not a cloud in sight. The ideal setting for love, I thought to myself.

"Good morning, and a happy Easter to you all," Father George said, greeting us near the church entrance.

"Happy Easter to you as well, Father," my parents replied, as we followed the usher to our seats.

My family and I were sitting on the left side of the isle in church. While seated just across from us were Abraham and his family. Mary, sitting between her mother and Ishtar, began looking over at me and smiling.

The two sisters kept no secrets from one another, though neither did my brothers and I. As I sat patiently listening to Father George, I secretly hoped the sermon would end quickly, allowing Ishtar and I to rendezvous as agreed.

"Aren't you going to be late?" Peter whispered.

"Shut up," Robert replied, elbowing him.

I joined in and subtly pinched Peter, who was trapped between Robert and me, "Are you crazy?" I answered quietly, looking around to ensure nobody was suspicious.

My brothers encouraged me to pursue Ishtar. Being aware of my feelings for her, they were sincerely happy for me. I constantly spoke about her beauty and how much I loved her. However, our families' rivalry was becoming a difficult obstacle to overcome.

Ishtar and I agreed, as long as we remained in the village, the hope of spending our lives together would never come to fruition – it would remain but a foolish dream of young love.

Though we fought the urge, we discussed the option of eloping. I had concocted an escape route from the prison our parents had created for us. We'd head south a few towns over and get married in a private ceremony. At least we'd raise our children without the burden of pleasing our stubborn fathers.

The fact that the love of my life was sitting only a few feet away from me made it extremely difficult to wait patiently. This girl that holds my heart in her hand, and my happiness within her smile, was just out of reach. I imagined holding her in my arms, loving her, and making her mine.

I wanted to stand up and shout at the top of my lungs that I adored her, and nothing would keep us apart. I ached all over at the thought of taking her by the hand, standing at the altar, and pledging my eternal love.

I started to believe that it was all wishful thinking to begin with. Our dreams were too good to be true. We needed to focus on our education as our way out of this village, I figured. I aspired to become a scientist, or an architectural engineer. I had no desire to remain in my parent's village with my future wife and no plans on raising a family under constant threat of harm.

There was no future here for me, I had outgrown Shaqlawa. I planned on taking the only beautiful person I knew with me, when I did leave. I imagined my wife and children sitting next to me on a beach, in a distant land, far away from the hate that separated our two families from reaching happiness.

As mass was concluding, I knew it wouldn't be much

longer that we'd be forced to hide our dreams and desires from the world.

I needed to be cautious and slip past my parents, Ishtar's parents, Father George, and of course, my brothers – without getting caught. I understood that one error, one wrong move, and my fate would be all but sealed.

Ishtar was waiting for my signal to sneak out and wait under the tree of love. I was to follow her, not too long afterwards, and spend the entire afternoon together. We both understood the punishment we undoubtedly would face for our actions. Yet, we welcomed the consequences of our love and prepared for the worse.

Chapter 8

I turned to seize each opportunity I was afforded, to absorb the beauty that carried my dreams in her eyes. Mary noticed my behavior as well and smiled back at me. I kept my attention on Father George, to avoid arousing any suspicion. However, Mary continued staring at me - as if she enjoyed the danger of getting caught.

I noticed Ishtar giving Mary a look that either meant, *shut up, we're in church,* or she was having some sort of *mental episode.* Peter and Robert were now aware of the activity that was brewing, right under our father's nose.

I desperately wanted to tell my family about my feelings for Ishtar, but I was too afraid of the consequences. Seeing as I was raised on the belief there shouldn't be any secrets amongst family, only made my situation worse.

Though my father had a reason to despise Abraham, and a good reason I may add, it simply wasn't enough to prevent me from pursuing the love of my life – not in my opinion.

Father George attempted to broker a peaceful resolution between our families. However, like I mentioned before, my father was a proud and stubborn man. I reminded myself that Abraham did attempt to ruin my old man's reputation and honor. In my heart, I didn't believe my dad would ever forgive what happened – leaving our families as eternal enemies.

I noticed my father following my wandering eyes, most likely hoping I'd lead him to the source of my distraction. I knew he was no fool, and was sure to discover what was happening. However, if he was absolutely certain of a relationship between Ishtar and me, I'd be dead already.

It would kill my father if I dated, let alone married, the daughter of the man who tarnished his reputation. In my culture, that's adding insult to injury. My dad would certainly raise hell – even in church.

My mother on the other hand was quite the opposite. She was kind, forgiving, and much more rational than my father. My mom and Helen continued their relationship, despite their husband's rivalry. Although there were forced to be discrete, nevertheless, they remained friends.

Our mothers have been covertly trying to mend the wounds suffered by both families. They pursued a peaceful resolution to this misunderstanding. Nonetheless, I still tremble at the notion my father discovers my love for Ishtar through the grapevine – the daughter of his enemy, no less.

The punishment would be severe, possibly being evicted from my home, essentially being disowned, I imagined. He'd invent cruel and inhumane ways of punishing me. Consequences that would make being homeless a more civil alternative. My poor mother wouldn't be able to save me from his wrath.

"Paul, get up," Peter whispered, as he stood up to join the line.

I snapped out of my thoughts, "Get in front of me Robert," I offered, frantically counting the number of individuals in each line. If I counted correctly, I'd be directly behind Ishtar when receiving our communion.

The congregation stood up and formed two lines on their way to the altar. Father George began breaking bread and blessing his parishioners. As fate would have it, Ishtar and I both reached the altar simultaneously. I, being a gentleman of course, allowed her to go before me.

"In the name of the Father, Son, and the Holy Spirit," Father George said, repeating it to each church member.

"Amen," Ishtar said, accepting the symbolic body of Christ.

As I stood close behind her, with the fragrance of my future invading my senses, a euphoric feeling ushered throughout my body. The scent of her being was holier than the incense burning in the church.

I fought the urge, with every inch of my soul, to reach out and touch the object of my affection. While my heart yearned for the cleansing that comes with accepting the body of Christ, and the Holy Spirit, my mind was dripping with sin.

I was glued to her every movement. "Paul – Paul, my son," Father George repeated, patiently waiting my turn to accept salvation.

Like a condemned man, whose hands are shackled by the ways of immorality, I crept forward. With my right hand, now resting in the palm of my left, I finally accepted my innocence – as well as my lust.

An overbearing feeling of shame baptized me with darkness, as I reached my seat. I knelt in front of my pew and began praying, solemnly and sincerely. I asked God to forgive my sinful nature, while also protecting Ishtar and me from any further trouble with our family.

I wished the rivalry that festered between our fathers would simply disappear. I hoped that God was as forgiving as the Bible promised. And I thought to myself – *for my sake, a bit more merciful would be ideal.*

I felt a bit desperate and pity for myself, so I continued praying. Is peace, too much to ask for on Easter Sunday? Is it a sin to love an innocent girl? Was I guilty simply for asking these questions? I thought to myself.

Am I wrong for following my heart, I wondered? To truly love someone and love her purely isn't a sin, I tried to convince myself. I opened up to God, yet, for a brief moment, I wondered if he'd punish me for being honest and expressing my feelings. I told myself, his only begotten son, Jesus, was above all – about love and forgiveness.

I was taught that Jesus' message was the truth, and because his idea of love was not reserved strictly for his people, but the whole of humanity, he was crucified.

I felt selfish complaining about being punished for loving someone, when my Lord, my savior, was punished for loving us all. I was in His Father's home, celebrating the love Jesus preached. I believed, since I was in church, what could possibly go wrong? As the book of Matthew 7: 7-12 taught, or in my case, warned: *Ask and you shall receive.*

Chapter 9

My only consolation rested in knowing I'd be with the love of my life in just a few minutes. The thought of touching her face or her innocent lips for the first time drove me crazy. The ideas that ran through my mind made my heart skip a beat. Soon, Ishtar and I would be away from the maddening crowds and hostile tension that surrounded our families.

Carnal desires continued racing around in my head. While I fought the urges, I finally conceded to the innate need to touch her smooth and soft skin. I pictured her smiling at me with those heart shaped lips, while I run my hands through her wavy locks, exposing that flawless face and those big hazel eyes. Her lashes were as long as the drapes that adorned a castle meant for kings. I was simply crazy for her; and soon she'd be in my arms.

I almost felt the heat emitting from her body. I imagined exploring one other, as lovers do. She was all that I can think of, both night and day. I was engulfed with emotions that baptized my soul. She remained on my mind, living near my soul and in my heart. I yearned for her so desperately that my body ached. I felt pain without her. There was sorrow within my soul that only she can remove - a void where love should reside.

I was snapped out of my lovely fantasy by my mother, who was now pulling me by my shirt. I wished, but for a brief moment, that I remained permanently in my dream. For those few moments, I had teleported to the future. A place I had created in my mind; utopia -where love and happiness ruled.

"Paul, mass is over. Your father is waiting for us at the front of the church," my mother said, as she finally stopped tugging on me.

I jumped out of my seat and rushed through the crowd of folks who were shaking hands and wishing one another a happy Easter. Nobody was in a hurry, as I was, to get out of church. They seemed content with standing around and catching up with family and friends.

"Have you seen Ishtar?" I asked Robert, though anyone's reply was sufficient.

"I noticed her walking towards the rest room area five minutes ago," Peter answered, surveying the church.

I was running late and didn't want her waiting for me. I feared she'd wonder where I was, or even worse, if I were going to show up as planned.

"Paul, mom is calling you," Robert told me, just before

I was going to attempt my escape.

"Now, Really?" I replied, shaking my head at the odds. I moved as quickly as possible without actually running in church.

"Yes mom, what is it?" I anxiously asked.

"It was nothing, never mind." She answered, turning her attention back to the conversation she was having earlier.

Great, if I wasn't late before, now I'm really late. But, I was determined to reach her. I was going to run like the wind; like the angels of God were guiding me to the heavens.

All my dreams and fantasies lay waiting for me on the other side of those doors. A few folks, about five hundred yards of grass, rocks, and a dirt road was all that stood between me and my destiny.

I noticed my father, who was near the church door, looking for someone. Typically, when my father is searching for a person, that individual is me.

He knows about my plans to rendezvous with Ishtar, I thought. If he stops me at the door, my fate will be altered. I desperately need to slip by without being noticed by my father, or mother for that matter.

This was it, the moment I had been waiting for. My father now was the only thing that stood between me and the love of my life. I knew if I were prevented from seeing Ishtar, my happiness would be replaced with misery. I prayed, my final prayer, before bolting towards the exit.

Chapter 10

*T*he faster I ran, the closer I was to realizing my dream. Gravity seemed to be suspended, like being captured in an out of body experience, I ran swiftly through the crowd. Twisting, turning, and bumping into people who stood by idle, watching me zip by. I was invisible, the wind was my friend. However, time was my nemesis!

Driven by sheer passion, my body contorted through the crowd like a man possessed.

I knocked over a little girl during my sprint. "Are you okay?" I asked, stopping only to help her back to her feet. I smiled, petted her head and was off again, without missing a beat. Nothing will stop me, now get out of my way, I thought to myself.

This was not a race in which I could afford to lose. Not

a contest in which anything less than first place was going to suffice. I had to win her heart. This was my opportunity. Fate was calling and I was determined to answer.

"Sheedana!" an elderly woman shouted, as I accidently ran into her during my self-made obstacle course that was, incidentally, my church. *Sheedana* meant crazy, in my language.

I recognized my father had now, officially, caught wind of my behavior. I, basically, turned our church and Easter mass into the Summer Olympics at Wembley Stadium. He gave me a look that would turn any God fearing man back in his tracks.

However, this was no ordinary situation and I wasn't going to worry about the consequences. I was willing to pay whatever price he deemed fit, to reach my reason for living.

After Father George finished his sermon, everyone gathered to play the *egg game*. It's a game where you take the tip of our egg and attempt to crack your opponent's egg without damaging yours in the process.

I didn't help myself, by completely forgetting to pick the *winning* egg earlier this morning either. I knew I wasn't going to hear the end of this from my father. However, in my heart, it was worth a lifetime of punishment to embrace the girl of my adoration.

"Where are you going Paul?" Peter asked, as Robert followed close behind as well.

I continued moving towards the exit, "None of our business. Now get away from me. You're attracting too much attention," I replied, quickly scanning the crowd to determine my escape route.

"We won't tell mom or dad, we promise," Peter added, pacing me, step for step.

"I know you won't, because I'd kill you if you did," I replied, not sure if I was figuratively speaking.

"I'm happy for you," Robert said, as he trailed behind Peter.

"I know you are Robert. I love you for that, but I must get to her on time, as planned," I said, hoping they'd sympathize with me, "You understand that, don't you?" I added, to ensure my message was clear.

"Yes, I do," Robert replied.

"Can we come with?" Peter asked, obviously missing my intention completely.

"Have you lost your mind?" I impatiently snapped, "Of course not."

"Mom and dad are going to kill you when you get back," Peter said, antagonizing me as I inched closer to freedom.

I replied with brutal honesty, "I don't care," and kept walking. Great, I forgot to wish my parents a Happy Easter, I thought to myself, only compounding the list of infractions.

My parents and grandparents were both distracted with wishing members of our church a happy Easter. I finally managed passed the doors and down the steps of the church. I paused, briefly, to plan my route to our rendezvous. As I ran, I realized I had a few shadows chasing me. Oh no, my heart plummeted as I thought to myself, Robert and Peter are following me.

I continued running, pretending not to notice them. When I get back, I will lie and claim I never saw them, I told myself. As I continued sprinting, I realized that my brothers were no longer kids. I began to panic, as Peter gained on me with Robert not too far behind either.

I felt sick, almost wanting to vomit. My stomach twisted inside me. My heart felt like it was beating out of my chest. Sweat was running down my face and into my eyes, my lungs were burning as if someone had lit a fire inside me. I couldn't breathe, although I was out in the open, I felt faint. I thought to myself, why are they following me?

My paranoia grew to a fevered pitch now. My mind, now scattered in every possible direction, was haunting me. Could my father have ordered them to follow me? Maybe to discover the reason I acted like such a fool at church.

I began thinking terribly negative thoughts. Were they here to prevent me from seeing Ishtar? She belonged to me and nothing, or no one, can stop me from reaching her. I thought, as I continued to run, ignoring the fact that my brothers were nearly side by side with me now.

I shouted at my brothers, while I kept running, almost at the point of tears, "Do not follow me, you are my brothers, but she's my angel. I would give you my life, but she is my reason for living."

I continued, "I would protect you, but she is my savior. You are my blood, but she is my heart. I pray for you, but I worship her. I am yours, but she is mine," I added, exhausted and discouraged.

They refused to obey my commands. Maybe they couldn't hear me, I thought, or even worse, they ignored me. Maybe they were pretending, as I did a few moments earlier, or they possibly didn't care.

If I only had that eighteen minute lead in this race, I did in age, I thought. That would provide me the advantage I so desperately needed at this moment. The faster I ran, the quicker they did as well. I was seething with anger, fear and frustration. If they only knew how I felt at that second, they'd stop trailing me.

My destiny, my fate, was waiting for me in the distance. I was approaching a crossroad in my life, a path that I must journey alone. I was on the threshold of going from boy to man.

I noticed the spot where Ishtar and I agreed to meet. I grew more anxious with each step I took. This was it, my moment. All that I imagined was now on the horizon.

"Not even God could stop me now!" I said, thinking aloud and for all to hear. Unfortunately, I didn't realize *he* was listening.

Chapter 11

Something didn't add up. Although I was running as fast as I can, I seemed to be getting nowhere. I must be losing my mind, I thought to myself.

It wasn't long ago, when I was given the duty of teaching my brothers geometry. The shortest distance between two points is a straight line and I could imagine where Ishtar is standing.

In school, I tutored Robert with his homework assignments almost daily. However, at this very moment, I regret helping him with his projects. He, too, also knows the shortest distance between two points.

I couldn't shake them from my tail. They, meticulously, followed me – unfortunately, I taught them well.

"Robert, stop chasing me!" I shouted, while I continued to run.

"I am going to tell mom and dad you didn't listen to me, like they told you and Peter to do, if you do not stop following me," I said, using blackmail as a last resort.

But it did not work. My brothers continued to give chase. I began losing hope on ever reaching my dream – alone. I begged them to turn back, plead profusely, but to no avail. Robert and Peter were as stubborn as I taught them to be. My lessons seemed to have paid off for them.

"I am your older brother, but you need to give me my space. I am tired of you guys following me everywhere, I want to be free!" I yelled, hoping they would believe me.

I lied about getting them punished, expecting it to deter them from chasing me. "I have placed you in trouble in the past, but you didn't realize it. I was the one who told dad that you stole candy from the market. Don't you remember the pain you felt from the beating?" I confessed, but they refused to believe.

I was able to glance back, while running, and noticed something extremely odd. The church was still within my sight, behind me, though I had been running for at least a minute now.

"Yes, it was me! Go away! Please, do not follow me any longer. I am no good, and I will only lead you to danger," I continued, however, my words only seemed to strengthen their resolve to continue chasing me.

"Peter, please listen to me. Do not behave like Robert. Don't pull in front of me, my brother," I begged, praying for a miracle.

"If you continue ahead of me, I cannot protect you. You must trust me or I will tell mom that you disobeyed your older brother. You will be punished and grounded. Please, you must turn around at once," I continued, glancing over at Peter, who was now ahead of me by a few feet.

I realized that threatening them was not working. I must try a different approach. We were taught to be respectful of our elders. Officially, I was their *elder*. I looked to my left, as Peter increased his lead. I glanced over to my right and noticed Robert, only inches behind me, catching up as well. My mind was racing as fast as my heart was now. I asked myself; *who is going to win her heart, if we all get to her at once?*

My insecurities were swallowing my confidence with each step. I reminded myself, or maybe I was trying to convince myself, that I was the oldest and she belonged to me. I continued mending my fragile ego by thinking; *it is a tradition that the oldest son is favored.* I attempted to grab Peter's shirt, from behind, to slow him down. But, I missed by inches, and off he went.

Suddenly, the earth shook, sending my brothers and me to the ground. A tremendous explosion pierced my ears. The sounds of people screaming and crying stormed a beautiful Sunday afternoon. My ears continued buzzing, as I tried to clutch them to ease the sharp pain. I felt a wet trickle run down both sides of my face. I looked down and noticed blood. The ringing in my head increased, along with the pain. Yet, as quickly as the chaos arrived, it was gone.

There was no movement. Instant darkness followed. A vacuum of emptiness surrounded me like a prisoner. I felt nothing. Like a voided dream. There were no lights at the end of this tunnel, only darkness.

It felt surreal. I was floating like a cloud. I traveled to a time and space that I had never been to before, an unfamiliar place in my life. It was peaceful and beautiful. Far from the reality that bordered me in my village.

I was happy. The pain was gone and so were any fears or concerns I had only moments earlier. I was effortlessly moving from one point to another. Like a fairytale, as I imagined heaven to be. A bed of flowers adorned the scenery.

I heard the birds chirping away. Finally, I was at peace – I thought. A bright light shined in the distance. I squinted, to focus, but I needed to get a better look. It couldn't be, I asked. Or could it?

Chapter 12

Although alone in the darkness, I felt safe. I knew my eyes were open, yet I remained blind. Was I in heaven? Did I die in that explosion? Were my brother's okay? Was Ishtar still waiting for me? As soon as my worries arrived, they disappeared. A feeling of euphoria ushered through my body, removing any doubts I had only moments earlier.

I floated, almost weightless, on what seemed to be a thick bed of clouds. I couldn't feel any of my limbs or body for that matter. I am having an out of body experience, I thought to myself.

Brief scenes of my townsmen, in a chaotic state, flashed before my eyes. I recognized a few neighbors running back and forth through the streets directly in front of our church - as if, I never made it past the road and into the field.

I stared at the familiar object in my sight. I envisioned a giant crucifix lying in the middle of the street. This could not be happening, I thought to myself. My mind must be playing tricks on me.

Quite subtlety, I found myself back amongst the soft comfort where fear ceased to exist. This was heaven. I died in the explosion and now I am in heaven, I told myself. I continued spinning slowly, while moving forward on the cloud that was my escort for the moment.

The softest clouds embraced me. I brushed my hand against a texture that was foreign to me, as I passed by. These cloud-like objects were warm and comforting, like I remembered my pillows being as a young child. I felt safe and calm. All my troubles and concerns had become a distant memory – no longer significant in my life.

I attempted to stare at the bright and warm flame shining down on me. However, the illuminating object was too intense and forced me to look away. I could not wipe away the smile from my face. I was absolutely happy now. Though briefly, I thought about my brothers and parents. I wasn't concerned about them. I just wondered where they were, I suppose.

I know they'll be safe in the end, I told myself. I knew where they'd ultimately end up, once their time had arrived. I looked around and did not notice my brothers anywhere. I assume they survived the explosion. I hope they were not worried about me.

Although I wanted my family to know I was okay,

another part of me took comfort knowing they'd be as safe as I was.

I remember my grandpa explaining what heaven looked like to my brother and me. Though, I must confess, this is not what he described. There were no angels, family members, or people for that matter. It was just me, floating aimlessly. Like this was my own suite, reserved by God himself. For now, I'll just enjoy the peace and tranquility of being in my own, personal, heaven.

I thought about Ishtar again. I hoped she was alright, as well. I still believe she will join me here, someday, and everything would be perfect – again.

Up in the distance, I noticed a hallway with many doors on both sides. At least my sense of curiosity was still prominent. That is more than I can say for my appetite, both for nourishment and the love that led me to my isolated fate.

I entered the hallway with caution. Though I wasn't afraid of the faint cries, I was not familiar with my surroundings, and I'd rather be safe than sorry.

I cautiously approached the entrance of the hallway. I wasn't sure which door to choose first; the one on my left or the one on my right.

I placed my ear against the wall to my left and listened. It was silent and only darkness seeped from underneath its entrance. A faint moan crept up from the door behind me. I quickly turned, hoping to decipher what exactly was responsible for that agonizing cry.

I inched closer to the door and stood silently. The disturbing noise subsided, as I remained still. My palms were now sweaty and my heart continued beating faster.

I wasn't sure if opening the door was a good idea. However, I was dead already. Nothing can get worse than this, well, almost nothing.

"Paul," I faintly heard, coming from behind the wall. I held my breath, hoping to identify the source. Again, *Paul,* I heard. The muffled and foreign voice, beyond the wall, sounded female. The noise almost sounded similar to a person choking on some form of liquid.

I contemplated answering back, or even something as foolish as opening the door. Although I was already dead, I still didn't want any part of a horror show.

"Paul," a voice whispered. Clear enough to decipher. I froze still. My body, now struggling to breathe, trembled. The door handle rattled. Despite the fear that had now washed over me, an urge to unveil what lingered behind the wall tugged at my soul. A clawing sound, now accompanied the eerie hiss that resonated on the other side.

This was the crossroad that everyone spoke about, the proverbial, *light at the end of the tunnel.* I wasn't ready to move on. I had so much to accomplish, so much to live for.

"Paul," the voice continued. I must have faith in my lord. This was my test, my obstacle, to reach heaven. If I displayed the same faith in my savior, as he did in mankind, I should be fine – I tried convincing myself.

I took a deep breath, worked up the nerve, and touched the handle. I quickly jerked back, as the sting startled me. I gently tapped the knob to determine if the pain was from extreme heat or piercing frost.

After a few pats, I rested my hand on the lever that stowed my fate. I recalled my grandfather's teachings. Particularly a Bible passage; Psalm verse 23:4 - *Though I walk through the valley of the shadow of death, I will fear no evil: for thou art with me; thy rod and thy staff they comfort me.*

This was the moment, my destiny, I thought to myself. I took a long and deep breath. Slowly, I turned the knob. With the door unlocked, all that stood between me and the secret of life was patiently waiting on the other side. Finally, I worked up the nerve, opened the door, and embraced my reality.

Chapter 13

As I gradually accepted what happened to me, and where I was, I heard a stranger's voice call out in English. I did not open my eyes. I wanted to remain where I felt safe and peaceful. Yet, I couldn't shake the terrible feeling I had that if I opened my eyes, I'd be denied the tranquility I felt in heaven. I feared having to face a reality much harsher than the one I lived moments before the blast.

"Paul, can you hear me," the voice repeated. My eyes remained shut. Horrified at what awaited me.

"Can you open your eyes for me," the female voice asked.

Who can this person be? Where is my mother? Where am I? So many thoughts ran through my mind. Yet, the only way to receive the answers to my questions was by facing my fears.

I couldn't understand why she was asking me, if I can hear her. Of course I can. Why wouldn't I be able to?

I tried to open my eyes, but they seemed to be glued together. I felt the weight of my lashes, as I peeled them back to see the light. They were coarse and dry. The pain was now starting to settle in, like an unwanted guest. I did not respond to any of her questions. Though I continued trying to break free from the trap my lashes had set before me.

As I managed to escape my self-made prison, I finally saw the face responsible for the interrogation only moments earlier. Everything around me seemed blurry and magnified. The slightest ray of light hurt my eyes. I was not where I last remembered being with my brothers. I now noticed a brown-eyed brunette. She leaned over me with a bright light that shined directly into my eyes.

She gently massaged my forehead, "Can you feel my touch?" she asked, though I did not respond.

I attempted to touch my face, but my body appeared to be numb and my senses seemed void. I tried finding my face once again, but I was unable to move my right hand. I looked down to see what was wrong. I was horrified and baffled. I could not see my right hand. I felt dazed and confused. I began rationalizing what was happening.

I was able to move my left hand which gave me hope that I must be under some type of hallucination of sorts. My God, I thought to myself, this is a nightmare.

Something was wrong. The last time I remembered using my right hand was accepting communion from my priest, as I crossed myself. What happened, from the time I left church and where I am now? I tried, once more, to locate my face, just to make sure – but to no avail.

The nurse explained that I was lucky to be alive, "The vast majority of people, who are subjected to this type of blast, typically do not survive," she said.

I had no idea what she was talking about. What incident was I a part of? I remembered being at church on Easter Sunday, celebrating the holiday with my family. All the while, my mind was on meeting Ishtar under the tree of love.

I ignored the nurse, who continued asking me questions, which I was in no mood for answering. I know these people were only trying to help me as best as they could. These doctors probably deal with wounded soldiers on a daily basis. But I am not a soldier, nor were my brothers. We were just boys.

We did not join a battle or were part of an army or a resistance. We were at church, enjoying a beautiful Sunday afternoon that happened to be Easter of all days. How did we go from the most special Sunday of the year, to the most unholy days of my life, in a blink of an eye?

Chapter 14

"Where are my brothers? Where are Robert and Peter," I asked, looking around, as if, to find them.

The nurse stared for a moment as she stood up straight, "I will be back in a few moments with the Doctor hun," the nurse said, leaving the room with her clipboard.

I nervously awaited an update on my brothers. A few minutes passed by when a tall man walked in.

"Hello Paul, how are you feeling? My name is Dr. Fowler," he said.

"Where are my brothers!?" I shouted, both in anger and anxiety.

"Robert is doing well. He had surgery this morning. He is alert and recovering in another room," Dr. Fowler said, looking over his charts.

"And Peter, where is Peter?" I asked, anticipating the same.

"Paul, I am sorry to tell you. But, Peter died during the explosion. He arrived far too late for any help to be administered. I am truly sorry for your loss, son," he said, as cold as I can imagine any human could be.

"Died?" I weakly mumbled.

The tears crashed onto my cheeks. I could not breathe and my heart was in pain. I felt as if a piece of me died with Peter. I shut my eyes and held in my pain, as the tears rolled violently down my face and onto my pillow.

"A land mine went off directly in front of the church. You and your brothers, along with dozens of others, were caught in the blast," Dr. Fowler added, with a matter of fact tone.

"I understand you might be confused and disoriented right now. I have you under some strong sedatives at the moment. However, I will give you something to help you sleep and I'll check on you tomorrow," he continued.

"We will be in the other room, Paul. If you need anything at all, just buzz us and we'll be here," he said, as he and the nurse both walked out. Leaving me to grieve, in private, I assumed.

I never made it past the street and into the fields. I wasn't near the *tree of love* or Ishtar for that matter. It was clear now. I tried retracing the chase my brothers gave. When it suddenly hit me – it never happened!

I could not fathom the thought of never seeing my brother again. I wondered if he was in any pain, which tortured me even more than knowing he was gone. Tugging at my heart, I ached at the thought that Peter had suffered at all.

I failed to do what an older brother does for his younger siblings. I led Peter to his death. I should have listened to my parents. Instead, I disobeyed their orders and lost my brother in the process.

What type of man was I to begin with? Did my brothers not respect me? Did I not possess the skills to lead them in their eyes? I was angry and devastated at the same time. I lost my youngest brother and nothing will bring him back. That will be a fact that will haunt me for the rest of my life. My eyes lids gained a thousand pounds and forced me to rest, both my heart and my mind.

The next day, the nurse came in to my room and explained the facts surrounding the explosion that cost one of my brothers his life, "Paul, my name is Hanna and I am the head nurse of the ICU at the General Hospital in Baghdad. I want to answer any questions you might have and explain your condition," she said, while I remained silent.

"Although you might not comprehend the extent of your injuries, not at the moment at least, because you are under heavy medication. Nonetheless, I will explain your condition as best I can. Doctor Fowler will elaborate in detail when he visits you today."

She continued, "An Islamic group planted a land mine in front of your church. Someone from your community must have set it off by stepping on it. That is what caused you to lose your right arm and both of your legs," she added.

"Do you have any questions for me?" Nurse Hanna asked. I couldn't reply though. I was filled with rage and anger. I simmered and brewed like a volcano that was ready to erupt. "Your parents know where you are and they're on their way," she assured me.

How dare these barbaric animals inflict harm on innocent people, simply because of a difference in belief? They preach that their religion is of peace when in fact they are carrying out suicide bombings and attacking minorities in their countries.

Islam means, *submit*, in Arabic. However, I would never succumb to fear tactics. There isn't anything more their *God* can do to harm me!

Their *Allah* has crippled me, injured Robert, and killed Peter – suddenly, like a jolt of lightning, it hit me, "Where is Ishtar?!" I shouted.

Chapter 15

The Medical staff thought it would be a good idea if we shared our feelings with wounded soldiers who also happened to be in ICU. Communication was a problem, mainly because we didn't understand English too well. They found us a translator, an Iraqi citizen, who was selected to help break the language barrier.

"Amir Hanna will be arriving shortly," Nurse Hanna told me. I hated him from the moment I heard his name. He tried to be a kind and gentle man with us, but in my eyes and more importantly, in my heart, all Muslims were terrorists.

"*Shlama*, Paul," Amir greeted me with his broken attempt at Aramaic. I did not respond, not even a nod.

In my mind, the only objective a Muslim has is either

to convert or kill the infidels. They pretend to be generous and kind neighbors. However, their cleric's rhetoric is the opposite. Many of the militants are taught that lying to an *infidel* to obtain the upper hand in combat is not a sin, but an order from God. That type of behavior is widely known as *Taqiyya* or *Kitman*. With that in mind, I was not going to allow this evil man to fool me, nor anyone else for that matter. The Muslims were now my eternal enemies and I vowed to devout my life to fighting them.

My grandpa told us that Muslims are promised the key to heaven if they kill or die while killing an infidel - *nonbeliever*. What religion, which preaches murdering a fellow human, is legitimate? In our religion, it is taught that in order to reach heaven, a Christian must follow in the footsteps of Christ and those principles were clear: Love, compassion, and forgiveness.

"Paul, are you not going to say hello to Amir?" Nurse Hanna asked.

"No, I am not," I replied, refusing to even look at him. I wasn't sure if it was anger or fear that dwelled in my heart.

"Amir has nothing to do with what happened to you or your brothers. You know that, don't you, Paul?" she asked, hoping to reach me.

"Well, I hate Muslims and you can throw Jesus Christ into that bag as well," I spewed, full of venom, "I will not turn the other cheek. Nor I will ever pray to God for help because he is deaf! How many innocent people have lost their limbs and lives because of these so called 'messengers' of God? Cities are being bombed, people terrorized, all in the name of this undisputed *father* who supposedly loves us equally. Well, to hell with him and his heaven!" I seared in anger. Amir and Nurse Hanna stood frozen in disbelief.

"But God is good. God is love," Amir replied, trying to calm me down.

I continued ignoring my enemy, "What father would allow his children to be harmed when visiting his home? If God is real, than he should have protected my brothers and I. *He* failed all those innocent people who were murdered in his name. He failed Peter!" I struggled to say, my eyes swarming with tears.

I wiped away my pain and continued, "Instead, he watches while churches are bombed. Even mosques are being attacked and burned down by sectarian violence. It is not enough that they're Muslim, because it is common that a Shi'ite Muslim will kill a Sunni Muslim and vice-versa, just because they are not from the same sect. You consider this civilized?" I mockingly grinned, while a dangerous cocktail of anger and self-pity brew within.

"I am not trying to condone or justify any type of violence. However, I don't believe God has anything to do with it. Some people are good, while some are bad. They just happen to be born into religion, but that shouldn't reflect on the religion itself," Amir said, attempting to be wise. But I wasn't having any of his lies. I knew it was deception... it's in their blood!

"Get out!" I shouted, "Remove this terrorist from my room!" I continued, pointing at Amir, while staring at

Nurse Hanna.

Before he exited the room, I added, "Amir, I hope you step on a land mine set by your own barbaric people," I immediately regretted saying that to him.

Amir looked back, somberly lowered his head, and finally left.

It was all too much for a young boy to endure. I should be focused on my education and enjoying life. Instead, my world has been tossed upside down, I thought to myself.

"Be happy that you're alive, Paul. Be grateful that Robert is okay as well. You have a lot to be thankful for. This incident should serve as a reason to live life to the fullest. Like each day is our last," Nurse Hanna interjected. Visibly upset, she managed to fight back tears of both frustration and sadness.

I was torn between the anger that simmered within and the forgiveness we were taught to extend. The more dogmatic an individual is, the more close minded and prejudice that person grows, I believed.

"Live life to the fullest?" I replied, rhetorically, "How will I do that? I only have one God damn hand, and no feet! Each day like our last, you say? I hope this is my last fucking day!" I shouted, tears now cascading down my face, crashing onto the pillow below. I continued venting, "I wish I died in the blast!"

Forgetting my dear mother's adage: *be careful what you wish for.*

Chapter 16

My grandpa told us stories of genocides committed against Christians by the Turks. Millions upon millions of Christians murdered by these, *men of God*. To add insult to injury, the Turkish government does not recognize that such a crime was ever committed. In my opinion, it is no different than a person who denies the Holocaust.

It's the narrow minded individuals; the evil tyrants who use their imaginary *God* as an excuse to commit atrocities. How can the creator of the majestic heavens and marvels on earth, just sit around and watch this happen? I know how, I told myself, *because there isn't anyone watching!*

This is the *twenty-first century*, not the dark ages. We have sent people to the moon, while these religious fanatics are stuck back in 1915. I have asked myself, many times: *what type of religion asks their followers to harm a fellow human in order to find salvation?* I do not believe in heaven. However, I am sure about hell though, because I am living in it.

Of all the people that the medical staff could have picked, I got Amir who wanted to be my interpreter. No thank you, I would rather die before accepting a Muslim to help me. I am in this predicament because of these people. I demanded they find me someone else, anyone else, just not a Muslim.

A few days passed, "We found you a match, someone who speaks Aramaic and English. However, he is coming in from the United States and will arrive by morning to meet you," Nurse Hanna said.

"What's his name?" I asked, waiting to pass judgment.

"Charles Benjamin. He is an Iranian Assyrian," she said, "He goes by Charlie," she added.

I was curious about this man named Charlie, who claimed he was of Sumerian descent, "I am fine with Charlie. I accept him as a translator. But only if he is, who he says he is," I replied.

"He was born in Iran. His family moved to the United States about twenty years ago," she replied.

I was eager to meet this Iranian Assyrian man with an English name like Charlie. However, if he was a devout Christian, in my opinion, his hands were covered in blood as well and I was going to tell him the truth about his *God* – one way or another.

Chapter 17

*E*arly the next morning, at approximately a quarter after nine, a knock on my door got my attention. In walked a tall, handsome man, donning a United States Army uniform. His head shaved clean, as was his face. I noticed Charlie's shiny shoes as he approached me carrying a folder under his arm. However, the contents I could not make out.

"May I sit next to you, young man?" he asked, waiting for my reply, before sitting.

"Yes, please sit down," I replied, moving over a bit, allowing Charlie to sit down.

Charlie got comfortable, "Listen, Paul, I know how angry you must be. You're probably confused as to where to place your anger as well. I know firsthand about rage, especially when directed towards Muslims," he explained, sympathetically.

Charlie seemed like a man's man. He looked directly into my eyes and continued, "I will help you get through these extremely trying times you will undoubtedly face for the next few months, possibly years. I will remain by your side and help make this as smooth a transition as I can possibly make this for you. I give you my word," Charlie said, placing his hand on my left hand.

He began to tell me about his life story, but I wasn't too interested. I was afraid of investing any emotion in Charlie, in fear that everything I believed before the explosion on Easter Sunday had been altered at a whim and could happen again.

I promised that I would never allow myself to get too comfortable or trust anyone again. I put my faith in God and I know how *he* repaid me, I thought to myself.

As the days went by, I began to slowly open up to Charlie. He had won me over with his sincerity and compassion. I found out that he was born in a city, just south of Iran's capital. I often refrain from laughing at Charlie because of his accent. You see, Charlie is convinced he speaks perfect English – but he doesn't.

The Aramaic dialect I grew up on was derived from Northern Iraq. This accent is different in many ways from other areas which Aramaic is spoken. He also tried to speak Arabic to the staff at the hospital and his accent was even funnier than his Aramaic one. Needless to say, Charlie was beginning to grow on me and I was beginning to trust him. Besides, anyone would be better than Amir, I told myself.

"Traveling man, huh," I initiated, hoping to learn more about this Charles Benjamin.

"Yes I am," he replied, "I moved from Iran to England to become an electronic engineer. After a few years, I moved to the United States and have been a U.S. citizen ever since."

"You're married, I see," I said, spotting the ring on his finger.

"I am married to an Assyrian woman who was born in Iraq, like you. Her name is Samira and we have three children together, all boys. Ashur, Alan, and Nenos are their names."

"I used to be a part of a trio as well. Until some terrorist, who was following *God's* order, changed all that," I replied, instantly changing Charlie's demeanor.

"Why aren't your parents here yet?" he asked, though he seemed nervous about inquiring.

"They are burying my thirteen year old brother, along with the other, dozen or so, idiots, who, like me, trusted *God* on Easter," I immediately snapped.

"How was your Easter, Charlie?" I asked, sarcastically.

Charlie reached into his satchel and retrieved an electronic device. It resembled a gadget one of my cousins from America described she saw in a James Bond film.

"All three of my children were born in the United States. That's Ashur, Nenos and Alan. That is my lovely wife, Samira," he said, pointing to his family.

"What is that device?" I asked, curious about the instrument. Not so much his family.

"It's a palm-pilot. You've never seen one?" he asked.

"Nope, never," I replied, shaking my head.

"I worked for a major software company that provided support for the hospital laboratories and equipment. So, over the years, I have been keeping up with the latest technologies. Not to mention the pay increase and room to move up the, *proverbial*, corporate ladder," he added, while simultaneously pointing out different applications and options.

Charlie was brilliant with computers and I thought he might show me how to use one. Plus, I was intrigued by his stories of traveling around the world. Just like that, my interest in technology began.

"Can you show me how to use one?" I asked, despite my situation.

"Of course I can show you how to use a computer, if you are up to it, that is. You will be navigating from site to site, like a pro, in no time," Charlie agreed, patting me on the back.

In my village, we were glad to have a working radio, never mind a computer. Consequently, I never learned to use any electronic device in my life. We lived a simple life in my village, that is, until that explosion changed it all.

As soon as the subtle ray of happiness revealed itself, it was gone. A hopeless feeling washed over me like a tsunami. How can I forget that I only have one hand? Does he not realize this? Is he just mocking me? I need both my hands to use a computer. The sensation of joy was swept away by the waves of reality with each passing moment that I watched Charlie type with both hands.

Was *God* taunting me, I thought to myself? Could this be another insult, piled upon the list of crimes this *merciful* ruler was guilty of?

A person can only lose so much before quitting. My mother once told me that the quality of life was important, not the quantity. If that's true, than what am I living for? I continued asking myself. I have no legs, and only one arm. Maybe death isn't such a bad option after all. Perhaps I'll finish what *God* started.

Chapter 18

"You didn't die in that blast," Charlie said, randomly.

I paused, staring at him. I wasn't sure what to say, or where that came from.

"I know I didn't. But this is worse than death, to me at least," I answered, still unsure as to his motive for initiating this subject.

"No it isn't. Death is final. This isn't final by any stretch of the imagination. You have choices to make that will determine where you go from here," he said.

"Death cannot feel any worse," I replied, completely convinced of that statement.

"I'll let you in on a secret. There was a moment in my life, a crossroad, when I thought about committing suicide. Although I believe it is a sin, like the Bible says it is, I have a life insurance policy that will pay out a million dollars, back home," he confessed, his head lowered, no longer the confident man who I have known over the past few days.

We remained quiet for a few moments, "Why? What made you contemplate suicide?" I asked, though I was uncomfortable prying.

"The economy was tougher on my company than most. Every other High School graduate, with a twenty dollar degree, was now some type of computer tech. My company was downsizing, not to mention the pay for an entry level technician is cheaper," he continued. His mood now completely changed. I was beginning to see the vulnerable side of Charlie, as he had seen mine.

"The company I worked for, at the time, was acquired by a larger firm. Consequently, an overhaul of staff and employees soon followed. Why should any company invest in a fifty-five year old, who demands a higher salary because of experience, when they can hire a kid, half my age, for half the pay, and has a degree?" he explained.

"Why don't you get your degree as well?" I asked.

"It's not possible. Maybe for those kids living at home, with no responsibilities it is. But for people like me, with a family and kids, it's just not realistic," he answered, shaking his head.

"So I took the interpreter position the United States military offered," he added.

"What if you get killed by some *God fearing* Muslim, while you're interpreting?" I asked.

He finally looked up at me, with what looked like a brief moment of clarity.

"I never think about it, though it does linger on my mind. But, what choice do I have? I must provide for my family, that's my duty," he replied.

"I guess you're right. I always said that I'd do anything to protect my family as well, and you can see how successful I was," I said, my bitterness taking center stage.

"I'm not concerned, because I know our lord will protect us," he said, losing steam towards the end. Considering the fact that he was here, at a hospital, tending to the situation my brothers and I were in because of *God.*

"Of course he will. Like your *God* protected my family and those poor fools at church," I answered, fed up with this *God* talk.

I wasn't finished yet, in fact, I was just beginning, "You want to know what I think, Charlie. I believe that you are hoping for the best. However, if something does happen to you and you die, your family receives that million dollar life insurance. That way, you don't commit a sin, by killing yourself, in order to help your family. Everyone wins," I summarized. Not taking into consideration his feelings.

Charlie lowered his head. He quietly stood up and walked out of the room. I felt guilty for hurting his feelings. What did he expect? I am in no position to be sympathetic to anyone's condition, but my own.

To my surprise, the next day, Charlie walked in with a bag in his hand, "Good morning Paul. This is a gift, from me to you," he said, placing the bagged box on my bed.

"It's not my birthday. Even if it was, I don't deserve a gift after what I said yesterday," I replied, sincerely.

"Forgiveness my little brother; that is the secret," he answered, flashing a bright smile.

"This is for me?" I asked. Even more humiliated, considering how I behaved towards this good man, for no reason.

"This machine will be the gift that will allow you to achieve all that you can imagine. However, before that can happen, you must believe it could," he continued.

"What is it?" I asked, while opening the box.

"It's a laptop. It isn't new, but it will get the job done," he answered, smiling.

I quickly opened the box.

"Enjoy it for now, without placing too much emphasis on typing fast. By the way, don't worry about using only one hand. I've seen people who have owned a computer for years and only use one finger to type. You have five, you're already that much better off," he added, improving my confidence.

I put the computer aside for a moment, "Thank you Charlie," I softly said, "Thank you."

"You're welcome, my little brother," he managed to say, as tears invaded his eyes.

For the first time, in recent memory, I had something

to be happy about. Yet my mind was consumed by Ishtar, Robert, my family, and of course... Peter.

Finally, I can be productive, I told myself. I immediately began thinking of different programs I can create. It would help if I learned the basic navigational skills first.

"How do you like it, Paul?" Charlie asked, still wearing that illuminating smile.

"I love it!" I exclaimed, "I have already come up with my first invention!" I continued, as excited as a child who just discovered the wonder of imagination.

"Wow, two minutes into being the proud owner of a laptop and you're already creating programs," he laughed, patting me on my shoulder, "No wonder I'm out of work," he quipped, shaking his head.

"I can create a program that will translate Aramaic into English. Since this computer doesn't have that option," I said, configuring my settings.

"No computer has that option. Not yet, at least," he replied.

"There you go. I found my first invention, like I said," I answered, with confidence.

Charlie began teaching me the basics to operate a computer, such as: how to create a file, connect to the internet using different browsers, storing, selecting passwords, and so on.

After Charlie taught me the basics, I connected to the internet via the hospitals Wi-Fi. I was finally, even if it was in my head, able to leave my hospital bed. Only this time, I am able to travel all over the world, places that before, even with both my legs, I would only visit in my dreams.

My life began showing promise, once again. I felt optimistic about my future and what lay ahead. I had hit *rock-bottom,* and the only direction available was onward and upward, I told myself.

I had a plan, in my head, which was bullet proof. Nonetheless, considering my past, I should have ensured that it was bomb proof.

Chapter 19

During the day I would participate in rehabilitation procedures and exercises that would one day help me walk with assistance. While at night, I traveled the world via my laptop. Charlie was there to help translate certain words or sites that I could not understand. While he also helped with intricate system of the computer, both hardware and software, to ensure it ran properly.

I prepared for my daily rehabilitation classes, when Charlie walked in with a look on his face that was not promising. I felt something was wrong, as he approached me. I noticed his eyes were watery. I knew it wasn't good. My heart raced, scanning a million possibilities.

"Paul, I have some bad news my friend," he said, sitting down, while shaking his head.

"What is it Charlie, what is wrong?" I asked, anxiously.

"I was ordered to head south for another job. I'm going to be forced to leave you," he said, pausing, "There is nothing I can do about it. I am sorry my friend," Charlie continued, with tears streaming down his cheeks.

I reached up, with my left hand, and wiped away his pain, "You have given me hope to dream once again. I am terribly sad and I will miss you in my life," I said, while we sat in silence, both unsure of what our lives had in store.

"At least you can send me an email, from time to time," he laughed, trying to comfort me.

"I will never forget about you, Charlie," I said, knowing the bond we shared would last a lifetime.

"Take this with you, Paul. I am a Christian, who has endured many trials and tribulations. However, my faith in our Lord and Savior, Jesus Christ, has remained steadfast, as should yours," he said, as we embraced and said our goodbyes.

I woke up earlier than normal, the following day. I contemplated all that Charlie had said and done for me. My views began changing about God. I felt a certain peace I wasn't able to find after the blast.

"Good morning, Paul," Nurse Hanna said, walking in like a tornado, opening the blinds and allowing the sun to storm in.

"Good morning, Nurse," I replied, too busy to look up, as I worked on my new skill.

"Charles Benjamin left early this morning. He didn't want to wake you up. But he did promise to stay in touch," she added, while checking my vitals.

"Your mother contacted Dr. Fowler this morning. She'll be arriving later this afternoon," she continued, only this time she took a moment to glance over at me with a smile.

"Today?" I asked, tore between the anxiety of seeing my family, once again, and the burning questions that had yet to be answered.

While in the middle of my rehabilitation classes, Nurse Hanna walked in, "You have a visitor," she said, as she helped me back onto my wheelchair and taxied me to my room.

As I reached my room, I noticed my door was wide open. "Are you ready?" she asked, looking over my chair.

"I am ready," I told her, "As ready as I will ever be," I took a deep breath and she escorted me in.

My mother broke down in tears as we saw one another. I tried to be a man, by holding in my tears, but it was no use. I broke down and cried as she ran towards me. We hugged and sobbed together. I was torn apart, my heart was heavy and yet, at the same time, I felt relief. I was happy to see her alive and well.

After a lengthy embrace, and enough tears to fill the red sea, she began to answer questions that simmered inside me since that fateful day.

"How is baba doing? How is Grandpa Sargon doing? How is everyone?" I asked, in succession.

"Everyone is fine, they were injured, but they'll survive," she replied. Her eyes filled with emptiness.

"Tell me how Ishtar is doing?" I asked, no longer afraid of the consequences.

"I have no idea, none at all. I don't know anything about her or her family. I have been consumed with Peter's funeral. I don't know too much about anyone outside of our family. Your father knows more than I do," she said, her tone changing from pity to denial, and finally, to anger.

"I want to see my brother. They will not allow me to see Robert. All they tell me is, 'he is okay', and nothing more," I shouted, growing angry at the thought of being restricted from seeing my only brother – surviving brother at that.

"Don't worry about Robert. I will tend to him. You just focus on your rehabilitation, so we can go home and be a family again," my mother said, tears filling up her eyes.

"Please mom, let Nurse Hanna do this," I begged, hoping she'd spare me the humiliation of being changed, like a baby, by my mother – again.

My mother was an angel. She tended to my every need, around the clock, without any concern for herself. Yet, I felt terrible. I was ashamed of myself. I still wish the explosion had just killed me, sparing me the shame I was enduring. Each thought, related to that day, drove me further away from God. With each passing day, my rage and bitterness grew.

I went from being the leader, and future patriarch of my family, to an incompetent burden who was completely dependent on his mother. Like my mom had a new baby in the family, only this child wasn't innocent or full promise, but instead, was damaged and bitter. I was not soft and adorable, but rather hideous and mutilated. I was ashamed to allow my mother to see me this way, let alone... the world.

Looking into my dear mother's face, I remembered the happiness she had in her eyes. I was her pride and joy. Now, I became the reason her life must be sold into servitude.

I lost a part of me with each wipe. Every time my mother touched my body, I wished that *God* relived his only son's death, so that *he'd* feel my pain. Those tears of happiness and joy, my mother once displayed, had now been replaced with pity and sadness.

I wasn't afraid of God any longer, because he didn't exist. However, if he did exist, he failed at killing me. I told myself. Maybe it wasn't *God* who saved me from that explosion. Perhaps it was a different force, the real creator – the truth.

Chapter 20

My mother didn't care that strangers were present when she cried. I wish the same could be said about me. I shed tears of anguish and pity in the dark, in private, where no one could see. My grandpa always discouraged crying, he would say, *men don't cry*. He was only half right, because there were exceptions to the rule and this was one of them. I am permitted to mourn for losing a part of myself to the primitive behavior of Religious fools, I convinced myself.

I not only lost limbs, but a part of myself, when that explosion took with it the love of my life, Ishtar. I would never be able to applaud something that I enjoyed, catch a ball, or even greet another man with a handshake. Yes, I'll cry and they will understand. I told myself.

I spent the next few days feeling depressed and sorry for myself, but I knew this would have to end. I did not die in that blast, I survived, and I was not going to lie around feeling pity for myself. I planned on maximizing the potential I was left with. I still had a brain, to go along with one good hand, and I was going to hone my skills, sharp enough, to cut atoms. I researched the medical advances on such situations. I found the inventions of robotic limbs that were replacing prosthetics in some cases.

I knew it would be vital to learn the English language as soon as possible, which would be my first task. Then, with the addition of my artificial legs and arm, my disability would no longer be an excuse to stop me from living a full and successful life. I was going to achieve all that I had dreamt about before the blast, I convinced myself.

I must admit though, things were starting to look up for me. My rehabilitation was coming along well now. I also learned to get around using the wheel chair, by myself. My ability to find my way, to and from internet sites, helped me improve my online skills. I gained a tremendous amount of knowledge regarding my injuries. I even educated myself on the advancements achieved in the medical field designed to assist those who were in similar situations that Robert and I found ourselves in.

My brother and I accepted the fact that we would remain in and out of surgeries for a while. Robert seemed to be adjusting to the rehabilitation schedule a lot quicker than I was. We understood our stay here was temporary, which gave us hope for a better tomorrow.

I wheeled myself out of the room and down the hall, when I realized that I didn't know his room number.

"Excuse me," I said, interrupting the nurse who sat at her station.

"Yes. How can I help?" she asked, looking over the counter at me.

"Looking for my brother, Robert, we came in together," I answered.

"Room 108, down the hall and to your left," the nurse said, returning to her work, "Did you need any help getting there?"

"No. I can do it myself, thank you," I said, beginning my journey to see my brother.

The medical staff truly cared. They seemed extremely attentive and patient with us, while we recovered. I believed things were getting better.

I found room 108, but I didn't enter. Robert's doctor removed the final head bandages early this morning and I was pessimistic about the outcome. He hasn't mentally been himself since the explosion.

"I am prepared for whatever awaits me on the other side," I said, aloud. However, I wasn't truly convinced – maybe I'd never be.

Chapter 21

I turned the corner into Robert's room and noticed that he was snoring. Something he didn't do before the blast. I wasn't concerned though, it might be normal after an injury, I told myself.

"Everything will be fine. I promise you, Robert," I whispered, kissing his head.

It was early in the day and I wanted to begin my routine before my next rehabilitation session. I tried getting in a few minutes of browsing before they dragged me away. I was interested in software development. I found a site that offered a kit that can be ordered and shipped to your home, a self-help kit. Right on cue, the nurse walked in.

"Paul, you are not going to your rehabilitation sessions today," Nurse Hanna said, smiling.

"Why not?" I asked, not sure what was going on.

"A special visitor arrived this morning to see you," she said, smiling as she walked out.

Who can it be? I asked myself. Both, my mother and brother were already here. My father was still tending to things back home. Then, instantly, I was overtaken with joy. I knew who was visiting me!

"Charlie," I said aloud, "He is checking up on me, as promised," I continued.

I couldn't wait to show him how much better I was at browsing the internet than before. I wanted to explain how tolerable the stay has been because of his gift. It has allowed me to forget, though briefly, the situation I was going to live with for the rest of my life.

"You're going to like Charlie. He is my friend, mom," I said, volunteering information that my mother, from her demeanor, can't care less about. She has so much to worry about anyway, I don't blame her. I told myself.

I told her about his travels and business in America and she seemed excited for me as well.

"Charlie is my best friend, mom. I love him like an uncle," I continued, anxious about our reunion.

There was a gentle knock on the door, "Come in," my mother and I said, in unison.

The door slowly opened. My heart sank deep into the pits of my stomach. My mouth dried up to the point that I struggled to swallow the lump of tension that had set in my heart. I gasped for air, while suffocating in memories.

I was in tears. They lined up and rolled down my face

like a funeral procession. I felt an array of emotions; from anger to joy. I wasn't prepared for this moment. This was not what I expected. I relived the fateful day that changed my life. I looked over at my mother. She seemed detached from my emotions. As if she knew the entire time.

A ball of fire churned under my pathetic demeanor. I needed to satisfy the rage that dwelled within me and this was the excuse I sought. How can they do this to me? I was not ready to face this chapter in my life – not in this condition.

Chapter 22

She stared at me in silence. My family was aware of her plans to visit, I assumed. They probably kept it a secret to surprise me. Well, it worked, I was stunned.

Though, I must admit, a part of me was flabbergasted at the vision that stood before me. I was relieved to finally see the object of my affection. Yet a piece of me was still angry, ashamed, and unprepared to deal with this.

My mother kissed her and left the room, giving us a moment alone together. She didn't say a word. She moved closer to my bed and stood near my head. We remained silent as the tears ran down both of our faces.

"Hi," she whispered, in a trembling tone that was both soothing and heart wrenching to hear again.

I tried to reply but I was unable to control my

emotions. My words had partnered themselves with my tears. She flashed the gorgeous smile that stole my heart, so easily, not long ago. She ran her soft and small hands through my hair, allowing her tears to use my pillow as a bed to rest on.

"Hello, Ishtar," I managed to get out, trying to guarantee that I did not break down and cry.

"Hi," she replied again, maintaining her smile.

She leaned in and tried to hug me. I immediately pulled away. I didn't want anyone to touch me. I was not a complete man. I was missing my arm and both my legs. I did not want this beautiful angel touching such a grotesque creature.

"I am happy to see that you are doing better. I am happy to hear the same about Robert," she said. Yet, the smile she displayed a moment ago was now replaced with a look of pity and sadness.

"I am so sorry about Peter. The entire village was at the funeral, Paul," she said. The tears of joy were now replaced by the dark reality of my life.

"I do not want to talk about him. Please do not bring him up right now," I begged. I had not accepted the fact, nor was I over the pain, that Peter was gone. It was my fault and I wasn't going to forget anytime soon.

Ishtar and I spent the rest of the morning catching up and talking about things back home. I showed her how good I was at navigating my way around a computer. We browsed different sites together that she wanted to visit. I showed her all the amazing places people can go without ever leaving the security of their home.

"You seem a bit distracted. Are you okay?" I asked, hoping that she'd open up to me now.

She hesitated for a moment, "No, I am fine. Just overwhelmed, I think," she answered, her eyes now wandering away from me.

"I understand, but things will get better. You'll see," I replied, trying to encourage her to remain positive.

However, as the day grew old, the more obvious it became that she had something to say. I knew it must have been tough for Ishtar to see me this way. She probably felt horrible about my condition, since it was her that I snuck away to see on that macabre day.

I was finally prepared to discuss the explosion that permanently altered our lives. I was going to tell her that I was responsible for my brothers, not her.

I wanted her to know that if I had to do it all over again, I would. Furthermore, her ever-present love in my life made anything, including losing my ability to walk again, alright, as long as I held her hand through each step of my life.

"What is on your mind Ishtar? Please tell me what is bothering you," I asked, as she lowered her head and released my hand.

I smiled and rubbed her shoulder to comfort her.

"Ishtar, everything will be fine. We will get through rehabilitation, together. Once I'm done here, we will get out of that primitive town and move to a bigger city... or even out of the country," I said, continuing to console her during her time of guilt.

She did not respond. She kept her head down, as the tears streamed down her face. I felt something was missing. She did not seem comforted by my guarantee, as if she knew more. Maybe it wasn't guilt over my injuries. Perhaps *God* had another surprise planned for me – something bigger.

Chapter 23

"I cannot do this," she said, continuing to cry, while avoid any eye contact with me.

"Yes, we will be fine. I will make sure everything will turn out as planned," I replied, reassuring her that I was still in control of our future.

"No, you don't understand. I do not want to do this. I am too young and I cannot spend my life caring for your needs. I am sorry, but I did not ask for this," Ishtar said, looking away, her face growing foreign with each moment.

My heart sank, while my mouth seemed to be housing a ball of cotton. I felt a bit faint, as if I was in a dream. A desperate and terrifying sense of panic washed over me. I was at the mercy of her words.

"I don't understand, Ishtar. What are you saying?" I

asked, refusing to believe what my ears heard.

"I am sorry Paul, but I cannot do this. We are too young to handle this alone. I can't do this while I pursue my education and career. I want to achieve things, move out of the country, and travel abroad. I will not be able to enjoy life if I stayed with you," she continued, without a break.

"I am – we are, just too young. I wanted to tell you in person because I think you deserve to hear this from me directly and nobody else. You are a great guy Paul and I believe you will accomplish all that you set your mind to. However, it will not be with me. I will be leaving tonight and heading back to Shaqlawa. I will not return here again. I am sorry for what happened to you. I pray God remains with you and helps you through," she said, finally gaining the courage to spew this ugliness to my face.

At least she afforded me the dignity of staring into the emptiness that once housed her destiny, now an empty shell. A defeated spirit is all she can see, I told myself. Unfortunately for her, I wasn't in a *Christ-like* mood any longer myself.

"How can you say this to me Ishtar? I thought we loved each other? I believed you wanted to run away with..." I paused, how can she dream of running away with me when I have no legs to run anywhere? I thought to myself.

She looked away as I froze in mid-sentence. All the anger and rage that was brewing within me reached the surface. I realized my situation was, literally, inescapable.

Every dream that gave me hope was now washed away.

"I am sorry, Paul. My father did not even want me to come here. But, my mother and I decided it was the right thing to do. We should have listened to our fathers. They were right, we were not meant to be and they knew it," she said, trying to justify her ugliness by agreeing with our fathers.

I experienced a second explosion, more of an implosion, when she agreed with their opinion about us.

"Our love was wrong. Regardless, our parents' rivalry would never allow this to materialize into anything more than a summer fling, between two young teenagers, who knew no better," she continued, her poisonous words now spreading throughout my body, or what's left of it.

Like a man in rage, I exploded into a tirade, "Get out! Get out of my room! Get up and get out! I never want to see your face again! Get out of here and go back to your father! I hate you! I have ruined my life for a stupid country girl, who did not deserve my love! My father was right about you! I hate you Ishtar ... you and your father have been a curse in my family from the moment we met!" I shouted, at the top of my lungs.

She remained silent and still.

"Get out of here and never show your face again. Charlie was right! That bomb did not kill me, but it did kill us! Leave, now, and do not ever mention *that* tyrant to me again! You and your *God* can go to hell!" I roared. She finally stood up, crying, she walked backwards towards the door.

Nurse Hanna rushed in to see what the commotion was about.

"I want her out of my room and never allowed to see me again. I hate her with every bone in my body," I said, insisting that Nurse Hanna, who stood frozen in disbelief at my outburst, remove Ishtar from my room at once.

"I lost my youngest brother Peter, caused Robert to be handicapped, disobeyed my father, and I ruined any chance I had of leading a normal life. I did all of this for an unworthy, selfish, and cold hearted person," I continued, my rants becoming more and more inaudible.

"You and your crazy father belong together. I should have listened to my family. I wish it was you who died, not Peter!" I yelled, while the nurse escorted Ishtar out to the hall and with every second that passed... out of my life.

Chapter 24

I remained in bed over the next few days. I did not browse the internet, nor did I participate in any rehabilitation that I was scheduled to complete. I was completely devastated. Like a bomb had detonated again. Only this time, it was inside me.

Doctor Fowler worried about my health. My body was not reacting well towards the antibiotics or the treatment. The positive results we achieved prior to Ishtar's visit had now become a distant memory – like my happiness.

"This mental state you're in is taking a toll on your health now and we're worried," Dr. Fowler said, pointing at his charts.

But honestly, I did not care if I lived or died at this point. I was unable to see the light at the end of the tunnel.

To make matters worse, Dr. Fowler had scheduled a meeting to speak with me and my mother regarding the limitations they had at the medical center.

"You will require additional surgery on your legs. Some of the procedures cannot be accommodated by our facility," he said, sounding discouraged.

"It will be quite expensive to pay for. We're going to have you apply for aid. If approved, they'll cover your expenses. However, the turn-around time for a reply on your application will take at least ninety-days, maybe more," he added, trying to gauge our reaction.

My mother and I were speechless. Without any money, I would be forced to live the rest of my life without any limbs. The only hope I had in improving my condition was to get out of Iraq and head to a country that can offer prosthetics. Again, all of these procedures would cost me a fortune, an amount, I did not have.

At this point, I just did not care anymore. I wasn't concerned, nor was I going to stress over it. I told myself. Whatever happens, will happen. I don't believe that any miracle was due. I won't pray to God for help, as I would have prior to the blast. I convinced myself that *God* died, with peter, in that blast on Easter.

I spent the entire day in bed. I wasn't motivated anymore. I struggled to see any silver lining in my situation. I wish I could simply sleep my life away, I thought to myself.

The following morning, Nurse Hanna entered my room on schedule, "Not sure how you'll take it. But, you have another visitor," she said, catching me off guard.

"I do not want any visitors," I replied, afraid of my curiosity.

"You cannot just hide here for the rest of your life, Paul," she replied.

"If this person doesn't have two legs and a right arm, he can skip my room and visit someone else," I snapped.

"As a matter of fact, he has two legs and two arms. However, they're both his," Nurse Hanna smiled, "Who knows, this might be a blessing in disguise."

I was curious to see who'd visit me on Sunday. Most people are on their knees today, worshipping a monster who feeds on people's fears.

I heard a faint knock on the door, "Come in," I said, anticipating the figure behind the curtain. To my surprise, Father George entered. He immediately crossed himself and the air in front of me.

"Get out! Take your witchcraft and get out of my room. Don't forget your imaginary *God* with you when you leave," I shouted, my eyes bulging from the pressure I was exerting.

"But Paul, my son, I came here –"

"Your lies have failed me! Church and your *God* betrayed me," I cried, interrupting Father George, while he looked on in horror.

"That was not Gods work, my son, that was ..." Father George said, attempting to reconcile my pain.

I ignored him and continued, "I knelt down in front of your merciless tyrant, in his home, and instead of answering my prayers... he took my legs. I am glad though, because now, no longer will I bow down to that *coward!*" I spit my poison at Father George who tried reasoning with me.

But I was in no mood for compromise and I found no reason to think otherwise. I just wanted Father George to feel my pain and anger.

"I want you to deliver a message to your *God*. You tell him, in my mind and heart, *He* is dead!" I exclaimed.

Father George tried to calm me down. A piece of me felt terrible for my tirade towards a person who has been a living saint to our community. I told myself, he was an agent of that tyrant, willing or unwilling, a representative, nonetheless.

"You're wasting your time Father. I listened to you, week after week, teaching us to obey all of *his* commandments. The only place praying landed me in was the hospital, Robert in the other room, and Peter under six feet of dirt," I added, sensing that Father George wanted to reply.

"Did you forget? I got on my knees, prayed to your *God*, and he punished me for it. I will spend eternity in hell before I ever kneel to that malice monster," I said, this time adding arrogance and spite to my deadly cocktail.

"I will leave this bible here next to your bed. If you have a question that needs an answer, you can find it in the Bible. God loves all his children equally," Father George said, hoping to change my heart. Though his intentions were good, they were far too late.

Father George placed the Bible on the table, next to

my head, and attempted to leave. I reached over and grabbed the Bible.

"You forgot something, Father," I said, throwing the Bible at Father George, hitting the back of the door, and falling to the ground. A few pages flew sporadically around before landing on the floor.

Father George paused for a moment.

"God loves you and has already forgiven you, my son. He will always remain with you during your time of need and will never abandon you," Father George said, kneeling down, he gathered the pages ripped from the Bible.

He fit the torn pages back inside the Bible and placed it on a chair near the door exit. He looked back one last time, as if to say something. I saw sincerity in Father George's eyes. He was only the messenger, obeying his master. Regardless, I had no room for empathy or mercy at this point. I showed Father George the same compassion his *God* showed me and my brothers on Easter Sunday.

"Tell *God* it is too late. I don't need, nor do I want *his* love now. It is cheap and useless, like *his* words. You tell *him* when I needed him most, *he* betrayed me. I was abandoned and left with no legs. I lost my right hand too. But, that's fine. This way, I cannot cross myself even if I tried. I can't kneel to worship him without legs, even if he ordered me to do so," I quipped, as Father George walked out without saying a word. He let the door shut gently behind him.

How can he just leave me? I am not done yet, I told

myself. I have a million unanswered questions racing through my mind and no one to ask.

"God is *DEAD!*" I shouted, as the door shut behind Father George, "God is dead! Do you hear me!?" I continued, my voice subsiding, with tears streaming down my face.

I was alone. Nobody heard my call. Not my mother, not Father George, and not even *God* answered my cries for help. I felt isolated and left for dead. I've seen heaven, I told myself. Who knows – maybe this was in hell.

Chapter 25

I remained in tears. I closed my eyes, while I lay in a pool of my own self-pity. I was not angry at Father George. In fact, I just felt betrayed by people, like him, who promise Christians that *God* loves his children and will take care of them. Yet, somehow, *God* forgot that my brothers and I were his children as well.

Nurse Hanna entered my room to give me my daily pills. I can tell she was concerned that my temper and mood had been drastically different, much worse since the visit from Ishtar and Father George.

"Paul, this temper of yours, along with your attitude, is physically affecting you now. We are worried about you. We suggest you see a therapist at least once a week," Nurse Hanna said, handing me a cup of water, while I took my daily pills.

"I am not seeing any therapist. I don't care what you or anyone else thinks about my attitude or temper. If you don't like me, you can leave as well. I don't need you, just like I did not need Father George!" I shouted, as Nurse Hanna walked towards the exit.

On her way out, she spotted the Bible that Father George left behind, "What do you want me to do with this?" Nurse Hanna said, embracing it with both hands.

"Throw it in the garbage where it belongs," I replied, staring up at the ceiling.

As nurse Hanna attempted to leave, an envelope fell out of the Bible.

"What is that?" I curiously asked. Father George must have purposely left it for me to read, I thought to myself.

Nurse Hanna bent down and retrieved the envelope, "This is addressed to you, from Father George," she said, turning the envelope over, as if, to inspect it.

"I don't want it. I don't want anything from *God* or his blind slaves," I demanded, ignoring Nurse Hanna.

"Well, I will take the bible with me and give it to someone who will read it. But I will leave this envelope here next to you, just in case you change your mind. If you are not curious, you can throw it away yourself, when you are ready to do so, of course," she said, a bit annoyed, yet preserving the kindness Nurse Hanna has always displayed when dealing with me.

I stared at the envelope, which lay on the table next to my head. I repeatedly read the message: *To Paul, from Father George.* I was curious to find out what the letter contained. However, at this point, I was not sure if it mattered. I thought about it for a few moments and finally decided to give in to the temptation.

I opened the envelope and took out the one page letter that was inside. It read as follows:

February 21, 2010

To my beloved brother in Christ,

After hearing about your feelings towards God, I was not too confident that you'd want to speak to me or any man wearing the cloth. So I chose to write this letter to you instead. At the event that you reject any type of conversation with me, you can, at the very least, learn why I visited you in the first place.

I heard of a fraternal organization in the United States of America, who founded a charitable hospital called the Shriners Hospitals for Children, which provides the highest quality medical care to children in your situation without any costs to you. However, they do not provide transportation funds to patients overseas.

But, I have additional good news; I found a special fund that was created by a philanthropist who resides in the United States who also served as the Vice-Chairman of Shriners Hospitals for Children-Los Angeles.

This gentleman, by the name of Al Davidson, has created the Patient Transportation Fund. He formed the PTF to provide transportation for children in war-torn countries who required medical attention.

Per my communication with Mr. Davidson, this hospital, in America, has agreed to accept you as a patient. Your application, for admission, is pending. Once approved, it will enable you to fly to Los Angeles, California, to receive the proper care.

I hoped to give you this blessing in person, but if you are reading this, than it is safe to assume that I failed you. I was not able to soften your heart and show you just how much God loves you.

I have left the application with Doctor Fowler. The application is already filled out. Both you and your mother must simply sign the authorization and return it to your doctor.

In faith and blessings in Christ

Father George

I couldn't breathe. My heart now resided in my throat, "Nurse Hanna!" I whimpered, repeatedly – but to no avail.

Chapter 26

I wasn't sure what to do with this new revelation. I was confused, hopeful, and terrified – all at once. I had so many burning questions, yet, no one to answer them. I wanted some type of sign, a hint from *God*, showing me what to do. Why is everything such a mystery, a riddle? I asked myself.

Tears poured down my cheeks. I simply could not take it anymore, "God, why are you torturing me this way? Are you not content with my arm and legs? My youngest brother's life did not quench your thirst for blood? Are you not satisfied with turning Ishtar against me? Can your lust for misery ever be quelled? What more do you want!" I shouted, staring at the ceiling in hopes that *he* would answer me.

I continued, "Why won't you talk to me? Why can't

you give me a sign? Why do you refuse to answer my questions?" I clutched the envelope and the letter it contained to my chest, as I cried myself to sleep.

I woke up a few minutes before midnight. I must have fallen asleep. I was mentally exhausted, while my eyes were swollen from the crying earlier. I read the letter, again and again. I was curious about the Shriners Hospital for Children and this man, Al Davidson, who created a transportation fund for strangers.

I turned on my laptop and looked him up. I found several links for Al Davidson, Certified Public Accountant, in Encino California. While I educated myself on his background, I noticed that he was a member of *Shriners* and is a decorated Freemason. I wondered what this *Freemason* group was all about. I was going to find out as much as I could about him, the Shriners, and these so called – *Freemasons*.

Mr. Davidson boasted an extremely lavish resume and background. His CPA firm was one of the most searched in the Los Angeles area, with dozens upon dozens of positive reviews posted about his integrity and compassion. From what I gathered online, he has been a respected CPA for over thirty years now.

Many of the links I found were videos of him, and a few others, spending time with disabled children at various places. I guess he was a member of the Shriners board or something.

I spent over two hours going through different links on Al Davidson. Many of them led me to a site called *YouTube*. And, while only briefly, I found refuge from my situation and caught up in the generosity of this man.

I discovered that the Shriners Hospitals for Children was a non-profit organization with twenty-two locations across the country. This foundation is owned and operated by a group called the Shriners international. From what I gathered, they cover all the costs associated with these children's medical needs

The Shriners Hospitals are widely regarded as, *the world's Greatest Philanthropy.* It is a Freemason related organization, in which members are simply known as *Shriners.*

I typed in *Freemason* and was shocked at what I found. They seemed to be some cult, a secret society, as some links called them. Men who worshipped the devil, interesting, I thought, now *God* wants me to fall into the hands of a group who worship Lucifer, wear strange outfits, and funny hats.

I must admit, I was intrigued. All of the conspiracy theories surrounding them were larger than life. From forming a New World Order, to the fact that the majority of past Presidents and many influential millionaires were all sworn members, all seemed far-fetched.

There were many conspiracies, and all of them hidden in plain sight. From the dollar bill, to the secret encrypt-tion on the pyramid, and supposedly, in Washington D.C., they built their nation's monuments to fall into a pattern, when measured, fits their symbol of an inverted pentagram. I wasn't sure what to make of these people, but one thing I did know was that I did not trust them.

Although, on the surface, Al seemed like a sincere

man, I wanted no part of his publicity campaign. A group of privileged Americans trying to pacify their guilt over making millions of dollars, while people around the world struggle to find their next meal, I believed.

I refuse to be the next freak show, or their next circus act. These clowns were not going to exploit my brother and me. I promised myself, I would *kill* these arrogant Americans before allowing them to take advantage of Robert and my situation.

I wasn't concerned about the repercussions. Nevertheless, what was *God* going to do? Send me to hell? *He* already led me into the Devil's den.

Chapter 27

I was still a bit apprehensive about investing any type of hope in Mr. Davidson or his Shriners Hospitals for Children. I'd been bitten by betrayal before and was too afraid to trust again. Especially if I was too believe in Father George and his *God* – knowing where that led me.

As I lay in bed, my imagination ran wild. Thoughts of the airplane, carrying Robert and me, crashing into the sea became so vivid that I smelled the salt water.

I fathomed the horror of hopelessness, as I fail to hold on to Robert's hand, losing my grip on him, and watching him plummet to the ocean below. I couldn't help but imagine these ghoulish thoughts.

I continued staring at the ceiling, replaying the worst case scenarios. I was exhausted, weak, and running out of options. What if I'm rejected, I wondered. My eyes felt heavier with each passing moment. I dosed in and out, struggling to keep them open. They narrowed with each blink.

Doctor Fowler entered the room and startled me. I slowly recognized that he was holding a manila folder. My file, I assumed.

"Paul, I'm afraid we have exhausted all possible avenues," he said, sitting down in the chair next to my bed, "I have done all I can do with the resources I have at my disposal. Like I mentioned before, you are in need of advanced treatment. Unfortunately, it is not available at this location," the doctor continued, as I remained silent. Both fear and hopelessness consumed both my mind and body.

He continued, scanning through the pages of my case, "I have done all I can for you and Robert. I will be forced to release you soon if you cannot raise the money to cover your expenses. I am sorry to do this. However, I recommend that you transfer to another location... possibly, out of the country."

"Some options are France or England. Of course, I was made aware of your people in the United States and I'm familiar with their organization as well. Now if you are able to secure the authorization from Mr. Al..." Dr. Fowler combed the page with his pencil.

"Al Davidson," I said, before the doctor located his last name.

"Yes, that is correct. How did you know his name?" he asked, holding the manila folder to his side.

"I did some research of my own on Mr. Davidson and the Shriners Hospitals for Children last night," I replied. Doctor Fowler seemed impressed.

"Well, I got your mother's signature this morning. I just need your autograph and I can send this off for approval. If it is accepted, I will arrange your flight with Mr. Davidson. Once completed, I will ensure you and Robert reach the United States," he said, handing me a clip board that was sitting on the table.

Dr. Fowler pointed, "Sign here and here."

I hesitated for a moment, thinking about the possibilities. I considered Robert's feeling first, who was now in a mental prison because of me. I owed it to my brother, if not for myself. I guess I needed a reason to accept a helping hand. Since I only had one hand left, my options seemed limited.

I took the clipboard and pen from Dr. Fowler. He smiled at me and nodded, "This is the right decision."

I had a million questions, but no time to ask. My window of opportunity was waning fast and I could not ignore an opportunity to correct my errors.

I was afraid of what all this meant. Either way, I was taking a risk by trusting these people. I wasn't sure where Robert and I would end up. Ultimately, I was blindly leading my brother... again – back into the darkness.

Chapter 28

Waiting for the approval of our application was merely added stress at this point. I nervously awaited the answer for Robert's sake, more than mine. As I sat thinking, I recognized a reoccurring theme: trusting strangers with both, my life and Roberts.

Almost two weeks had passed since I submitted my application. Doctor Fowler entered my room, early Monday morning, with a strange look on his face.

He stood over me and just stared for a moment, "May I sit down?" he asked, pointing to my bed.

"Yes, sit, Doctor. What is the problem?" I asked, paranoid and expecting the worst.

He sighed, "Well, the thing is... I know how important it was that your application be accepted as the next patients for the Shriners Hospitals for Children."

"They rejected us, didn't they?" I said, looking away, hiding my disappointment.

"Well, Paul, I am a bit sad. However, it's not as you assume," he smiled, "Soon, you and Robert will be heading to America."

"Your application was accepted this morning. I received the fax to sign and release. Mr. Davidson will personally handle your visa requirements to fly you to the United States as well," Dr. Fowler added, smiling from cheek to cheek.

My heart dropped, raced, and felt weak instantly. I was nervous, yet happy. I wasn't sure exactly what was waiting for us. No matter how many times I read the humanitarian stories about these men, I couldn't shake the feeling: *it was too good to be true.*

I was leery about these *Americans.* Despite being Christian, to me, they were strangers from another part of the world that had no idea what life was like beyond their borders.

"Are you sure Doctor? You've confirmed this approval already?" I asked, before informing Robert.

"Yes, I got off the phone with Mr. Davidson. He confirmed the next step was obtaining a visa. He is working on that as we speak," Dr. Fowler replied with a smile that remained on his face for minutes after the fact.

"What are the chances that my visa will be approved?" I asked, unsure about the timeline or the success rate of such a document.

Doctor Fowler smiled, "About 90% chance, maybe

even higher because of your situation. I wouldn't worry about the visa. Mr. Davidson seems confident, like he has friends in high places."

Was this true about Mr. Davidson? Did he indeed have *friends* in high places, I wondered. Regardless, I would find out if that statement was true.

"I will stay in contact with Mr. Davidson and update you on your visa status this week. You just sit tight and stay positive. Good things are coming your way, Paul," Doctor Fowler said. I tried staying optimistic. However, I remembered the same sense of hope had been crushed by Ishtar – not too long ago.

I wondered if this tragedy was my destiny. A life filled with disappointment and heartache. Or was there more? It seems like each time I repair my faith, *God* comes along and destroys it. But who knows, maybe there truly is a light at the end of this tunnel.

Chapter 29

While I waited for my Visa to be approved, I continued researching the medical advancements that awaited my brother and me in the United States.

As I researched prosthetics, similar to the one I needed, I wondered where we'd stay in America. We had some family, but none that could accommodate the extended stay Robert and I required.

Mr. Davidson was going to pay for our Visa and travel expenses, while the Shriners hospital provided and covered the medical care portion. Something like this would cost thousands of dollars. An amount, my family couldn't pay.

I grew anxious, but convinced myself, *these men must have planned ahead.* Any and all conditions would be satisfied before any of these procedures took place.

I was up early the following morning. I browsed the internet, looking for as many options that Robert and I possibly had available. I scanned through Mr. Davidson and the Shriners website to familiarize myself on what exactly they do and how long they've been operating.

I discovered that Mr. Davidson had posted many messages thanking the Shriners Hospital for accepting a couple of children from Iraq – not too far from my village.

I skimmed through the article hoping to see if there was any mention, by name, of who these boys actually were. Unfortunately, I didn't find any further information regarding the mystery kids.

Could these two boys, the article is talking about, be Robert and me? It couldn't be, I thought. The site even mentioned that the two boys would be greeted at the airport, before entering the United States of America for the first time.

My confidence grew with every column I read. I buzzed with excitement. The tension, waiting for Robert to wake up, was reaching a fevered pitch.

Either way, I was just happy that someone was going to have the chance at a full recovery. It just seemed peculiar that these two lucky boys were not Robert and me.

Chapter 30

The very next morning, Doctor Fowler entered my room at approximately a quarter past ten with a folder in his hand, "Congratulations, Paul. You, Robert, and your mother have been approved to travel to the American embassy in Iraq to pick up your Visa."

I was elated. I couldn't erase the smile on my face. For the first time, in recent memory, I was happy.

Dr. Fowler seemed equally as excited, "Your paperwork is being faxed over tonight. You will have your itinerary, which has been paid for, to begin your journey to the United States. Once you've landed, Mr. Davidson will be waiting to welcome you and your family."

He continued, "He will walk you through the entire process. Furthermore, Mr. Davidson has guaranteed all accommodations."

"I can tell Robert and my mother?" I asked.

Dr. Fowler nodded, "Yes, of course."

I still couldn't believe it. Terribly negative thoughts swirled in my head. Was there something I missed? I couldn't deny feeling as if something was waiting for me on that flight. I replayed the image of our plane crashing into the sea and finishing what was started on that ghastly spring afternoon. However, the idea of living in this condition was no better than death in my opinion.

The following morning, my family was driven to the United States Embassy, in Iraq, where we met with the officer in charge of issuing traveling permits. He stamped all three of our passports, without question, we thanked him, and moved right along.

"You will stay at a hotel for the next twenty-four hours, while you wait to fly to Frankfurt, Germany, and then to the United States," the officer informed us.

I nodded, "Thank you."

We arrived in front of this majestic building. It was taller than any I had seen in my life. My family had never stayed at a hotel before, let alone the Hilton International. I felt out of place, as if all eyes were on this freak with no limbs. I hated their invasive glares. A few guests in the lobby gawked at me with pity and charity.

I wanted to turn back, head home, and hide in my misery. I dreaded the idea of enduring a twelve hour flight only to be ridiculed and stared at by arrogant Americans. Nevertheless, I was willing to sacrifice anything to receive the computerized limb I had been reading about online.

Mr. Davidson didn't know my true intention. If these *philanthropists* believed they were going to use my brother and me, for a show, they were sorely mistaken.

Chapter 31

We were driven to the airport, by a cab, early in the morning. As we drove through the town, towards the airport formerly known as Saddam International, I regretted dragging my brother, and poor mother, into something of this magnitude.

I was terrified that this plan would blow up in my face. Since my ideas before, that my brothers followed, did explode... literally.

We boarded the plane first, because of our injuries, and I immediately felt this morbid and macabre feeling in the air. As if, this was staged to add insult to injury. Like a running joke that *God* was playing in my life and the only encore would be held at the bottom of the ocean.

The captain finished giving his instructions to buckle up and remain seated. I took the handicap seat with the window view. Robert sat next to me, with my dear mother in the middle. I stared out into the sea of clouds, trying to get a closer look. Hoping I'd discover the truth, or an empty sky full of lies.

The plane left the runway and we began ascending, closer and closer, to the *being* that put me here in the first place. I prepared for something tragic to happen. Each time we experienced any turbulence, I thought, *this is it*.

Contrary to Robert, who was as excited as a child, I knew what lay ahead.

As the plane settled gently into the sky, I stared out into the infinite sky and almost directly at the sun. I laid my face against the window, imagining my life without *God* in it. I wondered what my life would have been like today, had I not attended mass on Easter Sunday.

Why was I chosen to go through additional pain after that horrible explosion changed my life? Why didn't I just die like the others? At least their suffering ended with the blast. My misery seems to have been reserved for the aftermath.

I couldn't stop thinking about the plane going down. I saw the bottom of that blue ocean as my peace – my only refuge. The answer to all my troubles lied silently waiting for me thirty-five thousand feet below.

Chapter 32

I looked over to my mother and noticed her praying. I cannot explain it, but a rush of anger and frustration swept through my body like a lethal injection of gamma ray was shot directly into my veins.

"Stop doing that," I intensely ordered, looking around to ensure nobody noticed.

My mother ignored me and continued praying. Not too long thereafter, Robert joined her and began the same stupid ritual.

"Robert, why are you praying?" I asked, prepared to break his heart by expressing who I believed was guilty for all of this trouble in the first place.

Before I could truly begin my tirade, the stewardess came over, "What can I get you three?"

The airline was serving some fancy chicken meal that ended with a desert.

"I'll take it, to go," Robert said, pointing to the window.

My mother chose Robert's meal and drink. He struggled with making any of his own decisions.

The stewardess turned to me, "What about you, young man, what can I get you?"

Although I was hungry, I was too anxious, and chose to skip my meal, "No, thank you. I will be fine," I replied.

"I suggest you order a meal, just to be safe, in the event that you grow hungry in the next few hours or so," she advised. I reluctantly agreed. The stewardess smiled and proceeded to the isle in behind us.

I focused my attention on the ocean of space, outside my window, and tried making sense of it all. Why me? I wanted to wake up from this nightmare and find myself tucked away safely in my bed.

Did I ever hold a piece of Ishtar's heart, or was it all a mirage that only lived in my mind, I wondered. I fought with those questions, and many others, for the remainder of the flight, while I stared idly out... into space.

We landed in Frankfurt, where I watched many people exit the plane. About fifty or so passengers remained onboard, headed for the United States.

I contemplated all that awaited me in America. If anything good comes from this miserable journey, it will be the benefit of having a computerized arm. I'd at least have a future in computers. I was slightly relieved at the small window of hope I opened; even if it was only for the moment.

I was startled by the stewardess. I must have fallen asleep while staring out of the window.

"We are less than thirty minutes away from landing in the United States," she informed us, "Please buckle your seatbelts. Keep your chair and tray in an upright position."

My stomach ached, as my body tensed up. Though we were close to landing, I wasn't ready to face my future. That eerie feeling of impending doom still lingered beneath the surface.

This was the story of my life; a brief moment of joy, followed by a haunting amount of pain. This is what I expected. So far, *God* hasn't let me down – not once!

Chapter 33

*O*ur flight landed in Los Angeles at approximately 12:30pm. We were escorted out of the plane by two airline employees who wheeled us through the terminals and out towards baggage claim. I was not sure what to expect. I thought each face I saw was Mr. Davidsons. We continued weaving through crowds from one corridor to another. It felt as if we'd never reach the outside of this building.

As I journeyed through the airport, I was shocked at the amount of restaurants available in just a short amount of space. I began adding to the amount of hatred I had towards these arrogant people. My head was spinning, from side to side, taking in as much as I could.

Suddenly, I was greeted by a familiar face. He resembled Mr. Davidson, but spoke in a peculiar way. I guess it was Aramaic, however, it sounded different coming from him. He seemed happier to see me than I was to see him.

He knelt down, "Hello, you must be Paul."

I nodded, "Yes."

He extended his hand, before realizing I didn't have a right hand to shake. He immediately pulled back, stood up, and seemed quite embarrassed. He moved nervously towards my mother and Robert, greeting them. Only this time, I noticed he scanned Robert's body to ensure he had a hand to welcome.

I tried to figure out what this man really wanted. He was wearing a t-shirt with the word, *Shriners,* written on it.

We encountered an annoying and irritating delay through customs. However, Mr. Davidson spoke to the people in charge. A few minutes later, after a smile and a handshake, we were cleared and allowed through.

We did not have much luggage, aside from our carry-on. Robert, my mother, and I each had the one bag allowed. As we cleared the gates and into the airport lobby, we were greeted by an additional twenty-five or so people who officially welcomed us to the United States.

We pulled around the corner and into view. A silence washed over the faces of the waiting crowd, like they saw a zombie. I noticed the shock and horror in their eyes, and I grew angrier with every moment. I understood that our situation was harder to handle in person than it was in the pictures most viewed.

We became the freak show I feared we would end up. I

promised my brother I would not allow him to be exploited. I saw the pity in their eyes. The sight of two crippled brothers was too much for anyone to bear. The welcoming committee was most definitely not prepared to get up close and personal – not yet at least.

Mr. Davidson motioned for everyone to gather around, "Let's take some pictures together, before we leave the airport."

"I want a picture, too!" Robert shouted, holding up his hands.

A dozen or so pictures were taken with the crowd. We took turns posing with a handful of them at a time. I wanted to get back on the plane and go home. This was becoming as uncomfortable for me as it was for them.

Once we finally had taken pictures, we made our way towards the exit. I felt the eyes of strangers piercing at me like a dagger. We were not human to them, but some macabre show; lepers, for all to observe.

We cleared the sliding doors and reached the airport curb. A long black limousine had been parked and waiting for us to arrive. My mother shed tears of happiness, but my brother seemed confused by the gesture, while I was quite indifferent altogether. It looked like a funeral hearse, preparing to escort me on the long and winding road to a graveyard.

But, I guess this was supposed to make us feel special. Though, instead of feeling good, I felt shame. I reminded myself; *this was the sideshow that I was afraid of from the beginning.* I wondered what these wealthy business men knew about suffering and pain anyway.

I remained focused though. If they were going to use me for their personal gain, so was I. A little bit of sacrifice, in order to gain that electronic prosthetic, would more than compensate for the public humiliation I endured. So I went along for the ride.

We entered the limo and circled around a long road that led us to a freeway. I peered out the window, while Mr. Davidson was asking my mother, brother and me questions. I ignored most of them, allowing my mother to do most of the talking. I simply remained looking out the window, taking it all in.

I had never witnessed this type of traffic, and all of it in standstill, just waiting to move forward. Back home, only a few families had the luxury of an automobile. While here, in the States, it seemed to me that owning a car was standard.

I did spot a few exotic looking coupés along the way. Some were colored in red and one in baby blue. Even a jelly-bean green was not as foreign as one might think; not in Los Angeles at least. This culture came as a shock to me. Their access to such items seemed easy and abundantly available.

We finally arrived at our destination. We pulled over next to a building labeled, *Ronald McDonald House.* Before we made our way out of the limousine, a mob of people converged around our car, singing and chanting. Mr. Davidson stepped out first and gave my mother a hand. He then wrapped his arms around my brother, carried him out of the limo and wheeled him into the building.

"Can I help you into your chair?" Isaac, the driver of the limousine, offered.

I hesitated, "Please."

He carried me onto my chair and wheeled me into the building as well. We sat in the lobby waiting to be checked in. Mr. Davidson seemed to know everyone, like a celebrity, he greeted each administrator and staff member who passed through the lobby.

Mr. Davidson and his volunteers escorted us to our room. As we made our way through the corridors, I wondered how this would all end. I felt insecure, afraid, and out of place – far from home.

It seemed like the trip from the lobby to our room was going to consume the entire night. Every twenty steps or so, Mr. Davidson was stopped by a passing staff members. I began wondering if this man really was a celebrity. I stared at him with wild-eyed wonder.

We were being paraded around like an anomaly. A trophy he can add to his celebrity charity status. I witnessed laughter, cheers, and a jolly mood that was whirling in the air.

"Why are they so *God* damn happy!?" I wondered, aloud.

Not a single person acknowledged my statement. They continued on with the festivities. I am without limbs, in constant pain, my life turned upside down, and permanently handicapped... yet they celebrate.

We finally arrived at our room and Mr. Davidson unlocked the door.

I began humming, "Welcome to the Hotel California, such a lovely place, such a lovely place... plenty of rooms at the Hotel California, what a nice surprise, bring your alibies..." I sang, as everyone entered.

Mr. Davidson joined in, "Hotel California, what a lovely place."

I grinned at Mr. Davidson's singing; he was a funny man. If he only knew that I wasn't the clown in this show. To me, they were all fools in this circus we call life. However, I was the star attraction.

"This is it? Does this room come with internet? I will not stay here without it. Plus, this place is too small. How do you expect my mother, brother, and me to stay here together?" I said, shaking my head while looking over the room with disgust.

"Everything will be accommodated for. Do not worry about such trivial details, Paul," Mr. Davidson said, apparently offended by my abrasive attitude. He then waved at us to follow, "In any case, let's go out to the lobby and join the others."

I decided not to reply and reluctantly agreed to join everyone in the lobby.

My mother remained behind. She was in no mood to socialize. Mr. Davidson escorted Robert and me to the back yard of the Ronald McDonald House, where it seemed like a party was being held; a celebration with music, dancing, and food being cooked on a grill.

Do these people understand I am suffering? I contemplated. Do they comprehend the amount of pain I live with each waking moment? Shouldn't they be dressed in black? To me, it seemed as if they were celebrating my demise.

After what felt like an eternity, the party finally waned, the guests said their goodbyes, and headed back to their fancy homes. While my mother, brother, and I was forced to share a single bedroom unit. I had a million complaints. However, not a single one was being addressed.

I lay down on the floor, giving the bed to my mother, as Robert rested next to her. She pampered Robert more than she did me now. I guess she felt guilty over his injuries, since his were mostly head trauma, and mine were purely physical. I wanted them to be as comfortable as possible. I knew I can handle this just fine and it was them I was concerned with.

As the night grew old, I gave up on accessing an internet connection. My mother finished unpacking our belongings and I decided to call it a night.

I would try to connect again tomorrow. As for now, I needed to rest. I was tired and aware of the long days ahead of me. Plus, I was curious to explore the Ronald McDonald House when I woke up and I needed my energy to do so.

Chapter 34

I woke up bright and early the next morning... at least before Robert did. It was approximately fifteen minutes after eight. I found my mother already up and kneeling in the corner praying. I didn't say a word to her, I had nothing nice to say about praying to her *God* and thought silence would be better than spiteful words.

I turned on my computer and immediately searched for a Wi-Fi connection. My language barrier made the option of calling for help *almost* obsolete at this point. I was essentially at the mercy and control of my hosts, who felt more like my captors.

I decided, since I was unable to connect to the internet, that I would at least familiarize myself with the building and its amenities. I had my afternoon all planned out. Finally, some time for myself, with no show to perform, I sighed.

A few hours after I woke up, at approximately ten O'clock, Mr. Davidson knocked on our door and entered. He had with him a special lift for the handicap.

"We are going to the Shriners Hospital to sign you in, officially," Mr. Davidson informed us, "You will then visit the hospital daily and when you're done, each night, you will return back here to sleep," he added.

Great, I thought. More registering, more meetings, and greetings – which, by the way, I loathed doing. Mr. Davidson seemed more interested in our progress than I was. Is this for us or them? I wondered.

My mother pointed at Robert, "What about him?"

"Around noon, someone will be coming to take you both. For now, I'll take *him* with me," Mr. Davidson replied, gesturing to me.

On our way towards the hospital, Mr. Davidson suggested we stop off at some *fancy café* to pick up coffee. I guess this was his way of impressing me. Unfortunately, it would take a lot more than a drink to impress me.

We pulled into the parking lot and found a place to stop. I immediately noticed how many patrons this place had. I was curious to understand why so many Americans visited this shop.

Mr. Davidson guided my wheel chair and opened the door for me. A guest, who was leaving, held the door and Mr. Davidson wheeled me inside.

"What type of coffee do you drink?" Mr. Davidson

asked, with a smile on his face, "Do you even drink coffee?"

Does he not realize my age? Or where I'm from? We don't have a *variety* available. My village was content with just black coffee.

"I do not drink coffee, thank you," I replied, smiling, pretending to enjoy this charade.

"That's okay. I will buy you a slice of cake... two slices, and you will love them," he said, leaving me next to a fireplace.

I watched him interact with the people around him. He was extremely friendly and everyone responded well to him. I was going to reserve my opinion on Mr. Davidson until I was absolutely positive that his intentions were good.

He finally returned with his coffee in one hand, a bag in another, and sat down next to me, "Here, which one of these cakes do you like?" he asked, opening the bag to reveal at least five different pieces of cake. I understood being generous, but this was a bit too much.

"Go ahead, take one that you like. I bought them for you. We will save a slice for Robert and Miriam, as well," Mr. Davidson added, thinking about my brother and mother was a nice gesture. Maybe it was his way of showing that he cared.

While Mr. Davidson and I enjoyed our snack, I noticed a man enter the café and shake himself off a bit. It had drizzled a bit since we arrived. Mr. Davidson immediately raised his hand and caught his attention.

"Here is a spot," Mr. Davidson said, gesturing to an available seat next to us.

The stranger seemed thrilled, "Thank you."

Mr. Davidson offered his hand to the stranger, "Hello, I'm Al."

"Nice to meet you Al, I'm Firaz," they shook hands and smiled.

As they got acquainted, I again noticed the manner in which people react to Mr. Davidson. He seemed to have a genuine quality about him and people are attracted to it like a moth to a flame.

"What nationality are you?" Mr. Davidson asked.

Wiping away some rain drops from his shirt, he replied, "I'm Kurdish, from Iran."

"And you, where are you from?" Firaz asked Mr. Davidson.

"I am a Christian, an Assyrian, from Iran," Mr. Davidson replied, losing the friendly demeanor that adorned his face from the time I met him.

"Oh, very nice, we are like brothers. Our government in Iraq is working with your people to help them..." Firaz replied, as Mr. Davidson interrupted.

"We are brothers? Your government in Iraq is helping my people you say?" Mr. Davidson sneered. His friendly face now looked unforgiving and furious in a blink of an eye.

"Say hello to Paul. As you can see, he lost both his legs and his right hand, in an explosion. This is what your government is doing to help my community in Northern

Iraq, my friend," Mr. Davidson continued, with a fire in his eyes that could have lit the café at any moment.

Firaz sat stunned, his eyes now filled with confusion, "Sir, this is not the work of my people..."

Mr. Davidson leaned forward, simmering with anger, again interjected, "Why don't you come back with me to the hospital and meet this boy's younger brother who has suffered the same fate at the hands of your government."

I was stunned... taken back, to say the least. Earlier, I believed that Mr. Davidson was putting on a show, a charade of sorts, to impress my family, and those people who were watching him. In a single conversation, Mr. Davidson showed me, unequivocally, that he was sincere and genuine in his dedication to help my brother and me.

"Come back with me and prove that we are brothers. Support my cause at the Shriners hospital and Ronald McDonald House," Mr. Davidson offered his hand in unity and peace to Firaz, who reluctantly accepted.

Firaz stood up and embraced Mr. Davidson, "I will come back with you, because I want to know the truth about my government in Iraq."

Mr. Davidson and our new friend continued speaking about the issues facing the people of my land and the solutions in place to solve them. I studied Mr. Davidson closer, now that I was leaning towards believing that maybe it was his nature to help others.

I was not sold on that notion, quite yet. I'll need more evidence to convince me, without a doubt, but this certainly was a monumental leap forward.

Chapter 35

Mr. Davidson passionately insisted that Firaz indeed spend an afternoon at the Shriner's Hospital to get a firsthand look at what some of the children are actually going through.

Surprisingly enough, Firaz officially accepted the invitation and followed along behind us. Mr. Davidson was unusually quiet the entire trip back to the hospital. The emotional roller coaster he encountered must have drained him a bit.

We pulled alongside a building where Mr. Davidson stopped, "We are here, Paul. This is the famous, Shriners Hospital for Children-Los Angeles," he said, awaiting a response.

I hesitated for a moment, as I wondered, *this is it?* I expected something extravagant and fancy. I imagined a

Taj Mahal type of building, with water fountains and expensive cars out front. Instead, it was the exact opposite.

"Is this it?" I asked, staring at this peculiar building. I waited to be informed otherwise.

This just could not be it, I told myself. I dragged my family, all the way from Iraq, to end up at a hospital that looks nothing better than what we have in Baghdad.

I was disappointed to say the least. Then, reality settled in like an unwanted guest. There was no magic awaiting my brother and me. This was it, nothing more, no fairytale ending.

"Yes, this is it and you'll love it. This is the house of miracles. Now, unbuckle your seatbelt. I will come around and get you," he replied, leaving the car to greet Firaz. Who at this point, had pulled up behind us and waited outside his white sedan.

I dreaded the entire procedure. I just wanted to go back to the Ronald McDonald House and sleep this nightmare away. I had not been able to access the internet since I arrived, and if that wasn't enough, I have been dragged around like a dog on a short leash.

Nonetheless, we entered the lobby area, where I stopped and stood in awe. It is true, the old adage, *never judge a book by its cover*. Mr. Davidson was immediately surrounded by staff and people alike. I noticed a red badge they wore that Mr. Davidson donned as well.

After what felt like forever, Mr. Davidson finally finished greeting his colleagues.

Mr. Davidson informed the receptionist, "We're waiting for our chaperone to arrive and officially welcome this wonderful boy to the Shriners family."

She smiled at us both, "No problem, Al. Feel free to walk around and show..." she paused, "What's your name, handsome?"

"Paul," I answered.

"I have a brother by that name. Al, as always, please feel free to roam," she added.

While waiting for our escort to arrive, I saw some children in the lobby area as well. These children seemed to be in worse condition than I was. Yet, they were only accompanied by a parent, while I received the *Red Carpet* treatment.

Some children were missing limbs, while others had burns that covered their face and body, and others that had a cleft in their upper lip. It is funny how places like this, surrounded by afflicted children, like myself, makes one forget about their own problems.

I was ashamed of myself. Here I was, benefiting from the tremendous amount of support I received from Mr. Davidson, yet, behaving far worse than patients who were, essentially, alone.

A young girl, who must have been at least my age, sat in a wheel chair, similar to mine, only she was handicapped from the neck down.

Mr. Davidson noticed my curiosity, "Cerebral palsy," he said, "That's her condition."

I had never heard of that illness. I couldn't turn away,

as I watched her mother wipe her mouth and shirt constantly.

The poor girl seemed hopeless. It was a sobering few minutes in the lobby, to say the least. I began believing that my condition had a remedy and the idea of rehabilitation was not too far-fetched.

My eyes scanned the room. I watched child after child, my age and younger, handle their condition with dignity and courage, while I behaved cowardly. I vowed to handle my situation with integrity. Although those barbarians took my limbs from me, in the explosion, they would not take away my dignity.

I noticed Mr. Davidson combing the room as well. Tears swelled in his eyes, as they did at the airport when Robert and I arrived. At the same time, a lovely lady approached us with a smile that could light up an entire room.

"Hello Al, so great to see you again, my friend," she said. Turning her attention to me and with a smile that made my heart race, "You must be Paul."

"Hello my dear, so nice to see you again. And yes, this is my brave new soldier," Mr. Davidson replied, placing his hand on my shoulder.

"Hello Paul, so very nice to meet your acquaintance," kneeling down, she held my left hand, "My name is Evelyn."

Her hands were soft and warm at the touch. She radiated compassion, or maybe it was the fact that she was so beautiful in my eyes.

"Hello, I am good," I replied, my English minimal and broken at best. I was embarrassed, but happy to be near her.

She began speaking Arabic, "Do you understand me?"

I nodded, "Yes."

"Great, we can communicate easier this way," she said.

I wasn't comfortable speaking Arabic, "I don't want to speak this language. I don't want anything to do with Arabs or Muslims. I am here because of them."

Mr. Davidson interjected, "I don't understand Arabic too well, but, I know he is not too fond of Muslims."

Learning Arabic allowed me to earn a little supplemental income to help my father. However, at this point, I'd rather starve.

Evelyn and Mr. Davidson discussed the process in English and I managed to decipher a few words.

Mr. Davidson tried his best to make me feel at home. He remained by my side the entire time. Not once did I feel abandoned. I was more comfortable with him now, than I was earlier today, and most definitely more than at the airport.

Finally, a doctor walked in, with a nurse, and informed Mr. Davidson that I was required to strip down nude to be examined.

"Paul, you can consider me an uncle while you remain in the United States. You have no reason, whatsoever, to be ashamed or embarrassed in front of me," Mr. Davidson continued, "You need to take off your clothes so the doctor can examine you. I will help you, if you need me."

I refused his help, "Thank you. But I can do it, myself."

I stripped down, as requested, when I noticed Mr. Davidson crying. He excused himself from the room. The nurse followed him out and began consoling him. I am the one who is stuck in this situation. I'm disfigured, and he needs encouraging? Then again, I realized this man was sincere. He felt my pain and understood my anger. But, if he was acting, it was worthy of an Academy Award.

Chapter 36

Mr. Davidson maintained the same level of enthusiasm from the moment we met. To see him breakdown, this way, was both disheartening and heartwarming. This man cared.

I pointed at the X-ray table, "Climb up?"

"Al, can you come here," Dr. Santos asked.

Mr. Davidson and the nurse both re-entered the room, "Yes, let me help."

With assistance, I was placed onto the X-ray table. Though covered with a white sheet, I felt cold and began shivering. Immediately, Mr. Davidson came forward and held my hand.

He pointed at the panel where Dr. Santos stood, "I'll be right there while you take the X-rays."

After I was finished taking my pictures, Mr. Davidson

and I moved to the next room. When the doctor entered, he spoke to Mr. Davidson.

"He requires multiple surgeries. Not just the one we originally believed," Dr. Santos explained.

I overheard doctor Santos describe the arm they had in mind. He then showed us an artificial one. However, it was not the computerized prosthetic I promised myself.

My heart sank in my chest. I felt lightheaded. I slouched into my chair with disbelief. I was devastated. Mr. Davidson wheeled me out to the lobby where a few friends and some volunteers waited anxiously for the good news.

Mr. Davidson joined the group and explained my prognosis. He went on about raising the necessary funds to help with expenses while we visited. However, all that dwelled in my mind was the conversation about the stupid plastic limbs.

I tried to get Mr. Davidson's attention, "Excuse me," but they continued on, "Hello?" I said, in English.

"Yes, Paul, what is it son," Mr. Davidson replied with a smile on his face, kneeling down to square up with me.

"Sir, I would never have come to America, if I knew the fucking doctor would offer me the same plastic arm I could have received in Iraq!" I shouted.

Mr. Davidson was now visibly upset, "How can you speak this way to me?" he asked, "In front of my colleagues, friends, and people who have taken time and money out of their own pocket to help you and your brother. How dare you? How quickly you forgot, huh?"

A few of the individuals who were standing around us tried to ease the tension. But, Mr. Davidson was adamant about letting me know just how ungrateful I sounded.

"You are acting like an immature child," he continued, "if you are not happy with what you are getting, let me now right now that we are wasting our time and I will have you on a plane back to Iraq tonight!" Mr. Davidson snapped, his emotions revealing both humiliation and heartbreak at my choice of words.

I remained silent, as I stared at Mr. Davidson and his friends for a moment. Mr. Davidson said good-bye to everyone standing around and walked out without saying as much as a single word to me. I wasn't sure what to say to the gentleman remaining in the lobby with me. But I believed that I should be angry and jaded, not him.

"Don't worry, Paul. He doesn't mean it. You just hurt his feelings. We'd never send you guys back without fulfilling our promise," Claudette, who was at the airport when we arrived, said.

But I didn't care. At this point, I felt betrayed by these men. They used me for their personal gain.

Claudette escorted me outside where we waited to be driven back to the Ronald McDonald House. She continued, "Paul, believe me, everything will be okay."

I nodded, "I know," though in my mind, I prepared for the worst.

For the next few days, my brother and I received no visitors, not even Mr. Davidson. Which, to be honest, had me concerned. Even though my heart was set on a computerized arm, from the start, I was not willing to give up on my future because I wasn't getting one.

I repeated, over and over, *I must reconcile with Mr. Davidson*. I owed Robert and myself an opportunity to lead an ordinary life – whatever *ordinary* happens to be.

Chapter 37

I wheeled myself around my new dorm, when a nurse mentioned something about a computer room. An area, designated for education, with an internet connection that was available for all the children who temporarily lived here.

"Here," she pointed, leading the way.

I followed her, hoping she'd lead me to another room with an internet connection. Since the connection in my room was poor, this was the perfect excuse to enjoy a change of scenery. There is only so much praying I can watch, before losing it.

I entered the computer room and noticed many different children that were smiling, laughing, and enjoying their stay here. All the while, these kids had disabilities that seemed, from a distance, far worse than my own. If they can do this, so can I. And there was no reason for me to lose hope... not in myself at least.

I found a space next to a young girl who looked like a normal teenager. However, we were at a house for children with ailments and I was not going to assume any different.

"Hi, my name is Jaime. What's yours?" she asked, sitting next to me. She had a smile that stretched across her cheeks.

I understood what she said, even though I was a bit apprehensive about my accent.

"I am Paul," I replied, with the best English I can muster up at the moment.

Jaime extended her hand in greeting, "Don't worry, there is nothing to be ashamed of here. We are all God's children, no matter what we have missing on the outside."

I nodded and with my left hand, we met, "Thank you."

Jaime laughed, "Thank you? You're funny," she continued, "The only thing that is important is what we have on the inside," she rambled off, possessing a smile that washed my troubles away.

I smirked back, "Nice."

"You have a beautiful smile, Paul. You should wear it more often," she said. "You need a password to log on. But, not to worry, I'll give you mine for now."

I was confused. I tilted my head, "Wear it?"

"Ha, very funny, it's just a figure of speech. You'll understand, later," she laughed.

I couldn't help but stare at this perfectly normal looking girl, with her big blue eyes, and her vibrant smile.

"What's that?" I said, pointing to her head.

"Oh... my hat?" she replied, gesturing towards it as well.

I nodded, "Yes."

"This says, I'm a survivor," she cheered.

"There you go, you're online and ready to surf the waves," she said, giggling and positioning herself back in front of her computer.

"Thank you," I replied, opening my browser.

"If you need anything, just let me know," she offered, typing away.

I could not figure out why was this girl here? She seemed like the text book teenager, well minus that ridiculous hat and that army girl haircut. I was always told that men should have short hair. Although my ancestors wore their hair long, some even wore earrings. Well, the kings wore jewelry to show their wealth and power!

"By the way, where are you from?" she asked, turning her seat to face me.

"I am from Iraq," I answered.

"That is nice. There are so many children who stay here, our age, from all over the world. I am from Tucson, Arizona," she explained, "My dad is in the Air Force. And when I am of age, I will join the Air Force, like my daddy, and serve my country. If you are nice to me, I might let you to take a ride in my F-16," She giggled, playfully bumping into me.

"That sounds fun," I managed, before she continued.

"My mom was a bank teller back home. But she took some time off to stay near me until I get better. I'm going back home soon. I won't stay here forever. Plus, I am tired of wearing these silly hats and bandana's. I want my beautiful golden hair back again. I miss it sometimes," she said, while pouting at me and quickly reverting back to her warm smile.

I did not say much. I just listened to her for a while go on and on about things she did back home, in Arizona. She was so full of life, so animated, and with each story, her face painted a beautiful picture of her emotions. I knew she was sick, but from just looking at her, you couldn't tell what she suffered from – nor was I going to ask.

"Okay, okay, I'll let you go back studying the cosmos," she chuckled and pinched my arm.

She was something else, I thought, and most certainly did not belong here with the rest of us freaks.

I immediately researched different prosthetics, unfortunately, only the non-robotic options.

I finally gave in and clicked on one that I believed was perfect for me. I was fascinated by its mechanics and felt anxious and eager to own one. Passing up the computerized limbs was a lot tougher than I expected. And with each search, more of the updated technology ads made their way onto my pages, I grew more irritated.

I leaned back in a sea frustration. I glanced over to

Jaime's screen and noticed she was reading some texts that were unclear to me.

She scrolled down and I noticed a symbol of the cross. There was a tiny picture of what looked like a modern depiction of Jesus Christ. She was reading Bible verses and wore the most joyful expression I had ever seen. I couldn't understand her. Here was a normal and pretty girl, with no afflictions to the naked eye, and yet reading a book that is believed to contain miracles, while in a building that housed the hopeless.

What was she so happy about? We were here because of an illness, or at the very least, missing something that other children our ages possessed. I stared at Jaime for a few seconds. She shook her head from side to side. She continued, silently mouthing Bible passages, while I followed along.

Jaime stood up and packed her belongings, "Well, it was very nice to meet you Paul. I am not too far down the hall from here, room eight, just in case you ever want to stop in and say hello."

"Okay, thank you. It was very nice to meet you," I replied.

Jaime walked out waving and smiling at other children and staff members as well. I continued researching the modifications for different types of prosthetics.

No matter how hard I tried to forget, there was just no way was I going to convince myself that this entire trip was worth the trouble if I only received some generic limbs.

A ring of negativity formed above me as I wallowed in self-pity. I wondered, how long before these clouds of darkness finally pour down and wash away all my hopes.

Chapter 38

I made my way back to the room so that I could research a bit more on Mr. Al Davidson and these Freemasons. I purposely chose my room, even though the Wi-Fi connection was fair at best, whereas as privacy would be an issue in the computer room. I entered the room, discovered my mother crying, and Robert nowhere to be found.

"What is wrong, Mother?" I asked, looking around for my brother, "Where is Robert?"

"Your brother is fine, and I am okay, Paul," she replied, wiping away her tears.

"If everything is okay, why are you crying?" I insisted, moving directly in front of my mother who forced a smile.

"It is nothing, really. I just am worried about you and your brother is all," she answered, brushing her hand through my hair.

"I love you both so very much. I just want you to take care of your brother no matter what he goes through. I want you to promise me that you will look after him the best you can," she added, looking into my eyes.

"Yes, I promise, I will care for Robert. You do not need to worry, at all," I assured her, conveying a look of confidence.

This episode of tears only compounded the anger that brewed within over being denied what I came this far for. I spent the remainder of the day lying in bed reading up on random topics. I did everything I could to keep my mind off how frustrated I truly was with this entire charade.

Early the next morning, I heard a knock on my door and my mother got up to answer.

"Hi ma'am, is Paul up yet?" asked a voice, which I recognized immediately as Jaime's.

"Yes, one minute," I replied, asking my mother to help me up and into my wheelchair.

"Good morning Paul. I hoped you join me in the English class they offer," she said, smiling, this time wearing a head cover my grandmother wore to church.

"Yes, I will go with you," I replied, grabbing my laptop. I pointed at her head, "What are you wearing now?"

She bounced around, circling in place, "It's my good luck bandana!"

"It was nice to meet you ma'am, sorry if I woke

anyone," Jaime told my mother, as we left down the hallway together.

Jaime wheeled me down the hall, through several doors, and past the computer area, to a nearby adjacent room. On the door, it read, *English, Second Language*. I must admit, at first I was a bit hesitant and even nervous one might claim. However, I was eager to improve my English. What better time to learn than now.

"Good morning everyone, please take your seats. To any new kids, you will be required to stand up and introduce yourself to the class," the instructor said, as we sat down, "My name is Trudy," she was a slender woman with jet black hair and a pleasant demeanor.

There was only one new student aside from me.

"I am Paul," I managed to say with a bit of tension in my voice.

Trudy looked over and noticed my disability, "Welcome, Paul."

Everyone kindly welcomed me, which made me feel important, even if it was for a moment. Jaime reached over, put her hand on my shoulder, and smiled. I sincerely appreciated what she was trying to do for me.

We spent the morning learning the basics in English. The teacher assigned partners to group up in pairs in order to complete our daily assignments.

Jaime and I immediately partnered together. Well, it was Jaime who actually jumped up and requested that we pair up, and the teacher agreed. Jaime's confidence and positive nature was a break from the negative aura that surrounded me. Though I feared asking, she did seem gaunt and her color was a bit pale this morning.

I was not going to ask her just yet. I did not want to make her feel uncomfortable in any way and it wasn't my business to begin with. If she wanted me to know, she would volunteer that information herself. As the English session ended, Jaime wheeled me back to my room.

"Do you want to spend some time in the leisure room just hanging out?" she asked, reaching over my shoulder, now staring directly into my face with her bright eyes.

"No, thank you," I declined.

I was a bit exhausted and annoyed from my inability to grasp the first session as quickly as I thought I would – maybe even embarrassed. Not to mention that I didn't want her to know my true feelings about her *God* and his wicked ways.

"Are you sure, Paul?" she asked again, looking over my shoulder.

"No, I do not want to go now," I replied.

She tried again, with her animated personality, "Okay, I think it would be fun and you would really enjoy it...maybe tomorrow then," she added.

"Thank you," I replied.

She wheeled me inside my empty room. My mother and Robert might still be with the doctors, I assumed.

"When is your surgery, Paul?" Jaime asked, sitting on my bed.

"Tomorrow," I replied, pointing to the calendar on the wall.

"Don't be worried, everything will be just fine. You'll see," she said, while lightly bouncing on my bed.

I wish I shared that same confidence she did. But, unfortunately, I did not. My mind moved away from the idea of a robotic arm, but my heart was fixed.

"I will come visit you after your surgery, if that's okay with you," Jaime added.

I agreed, "I will see you tomorrow."

Jaime strolled out of my room, jolly and full of life, bouncing through the halls that housed so much pain and sorrow. It was something to be witnessed, a building full of children, shackled with disabilities, who might never lead a normal life. Yet, this one individual was enjoying her life here, like it was some fantasy resort off an exotic island.

I was beginning to wonder if maybe she was off her rocker. I smiled, as the image of her dancing along the corridors with her hands swinging back and forth replayed in my head.

I was nervous about my surgery for tomorrow morning and wondered where the hell Mr. Davidson was? I was supposed to meet the doctors again today and nobody was here to help translate the information. I had learned a lot in my first day in English class, but what I learned was the basics, certainly not enough to sustain an entire conversation. I barely understood the doctor with Mr. Davidson interpreting, let alone without him.

Approximately an hour or so of my return to my room, in walked my mother, Robert and Mr. Davidson following behind. I actually heard them arriving a few moments before the door opened. Mr. Davidson causes quite the commotion, wherever he is.

I was in a foul mood, maybe it was due to the surgery, scheduled for tomorrow or not getting what I wanted. Not sure exactly, but it could have been a combination of both.

"Hello Paul, how are you today?" Mr. Davidson asked, opening a handful of brown paper bags with that fancy café logo on it. "Would you like some cake? I bought enough for all of us to enjoy."

"No thank you, I am not hungry," I replied, pretending to be surfing the internet for something important.

"Has the doctor spoken to you about tomorrow's surgery yet?" he asked, sitting down with my mother and brother, while eating their cake and drinking their fancy coffee.

"No not yet, I have been in English class since this morning," I opened new tabs, trying to look busy.

"Let me go call the doctor and figure out what is planned," he offered, heading to the door without even finishing his cake.

Mr. Davidson was dedicated, if nothing else. Once committed, it seemed like he'd invest all of his time and energy to see any project through. That is a virtue that I could not deny about him. Mr. Davidson earned a little respect from me after the café incident a couple of days ago. He proved that he doesn't just talk the talk – he walks the walk.

Chapter 39

M r. Davidson returned with information about my surgery procedure.

"Do you want me to sit in the waiting room, until your surgery is complete?" he asked.

"Yes, I would feel better if you stayed with me," I replied.

Mr. Davidson choked up with emotion. This reaction was odd to me. But I soon realized that Mr. Davidson was passionate about charity.

I must confess. I was nervous and afraid. I was not sure what was going to happen to me during and after the procedure. There would be no excuses. It was either live with it or give up hope. My entire life has been put on standby awaiting this surgery – this moment.

I imagined what my life was going to be like with the

prosthetic. I barely remember my life before this terrible nightmare happened to my family and me. Although it was only a short time ago, I could not, for the life of me, recall what it was like to be whole.

We go through our entire lives and never face such a harsh and damning reality. We take for granted some of the simplest gifts in life. Not until an irreversible tragedy occurs do we actually take a moment and appreciate what we are born with.

I was prepped before surgery. Mr. Davidson and my mother walked along side of me. I noticed his tears traveled down to meet me on my gurney.

We reached a certain point where Mr. Davidson and my mother were ordered to go no further. The surgery itself was approximately four hours long. The chances of success were noted at ninety-nine percent, as per the doctors.

They switched me from the transportation gurney to the surgery table. I searched around in hopes of a miracle. I had not given up on a computerized prosthetic. But as the moments ticked away, the shadow of reality loomed over me like *the calm before the storm.*

What was I thinking? My life had been a series of unfortunate events and this would be no different. I conceded any foolish notions of miracles or fairy tale endings. This was it, a cold and harsh reality I would be forced to live with for the remainder of my miserable existence.

"Count to ten, Paul," Dr. Santos requested, before I could even reach two... I was sedated.

I opened my eyes and found myself in complete darkness. I reached over to turn the light switch on, but I couldn't reach it. I raised both my hands and noticed that I was given a computerized arm. However, it was not obeying my commands, no matter how hard I tried; as if it had a mind of its own.

I was terrified and left alone with this machine. I tried screaming but my throat was sore and my voice could not carry. I started to panic. I lifted myself up to a sitting position and noticed the surgery room door swing open.

"Who is there? Mr. Davidson, is that you?" I plead, moving side to side, hoping to get a better view.

But the figure, a shadow in the dark room, was too short to be Mr. Davidson, "Mother, is that you?" I continued searching for the identity of the ominous figure.

I began rationalizing my situation. Was this some sort of gag Mr. Davidson was playing on me? But, this was no joke, I told myself, this is going too far. I am hardly out of surgery, at least give me a day or so to recover completely before playing games with me.

I contemplated the possibilities, as the dark shadowy figure moved towards me. I froze in horror. I could not say a word. My heart plummeted. A lump in my throat formed from the terror. I struggled to swallow a single breath of fresh air.

"Who are you?" I managed to whisper, while the terror had all but strangled me with its silence.

I fell back onto the table and almost resorted to prayer. I wondered if this was some punishment for

179

blasphemy. Was this the verdict rendered by *God* for cursing him? Could this be the angel of death coming to claim my soul?

I shut my eyes, and the silence remained with me for a moment. I lay there quietly before I finally convinced myself that this was worse than death. I gathered the courage to slowly drag my eyes open... nothing. I was alone, at least from what I can see directly above me. I had not worked up the nerve to look side to side yet.

I felt a presence next to me. I was petrified. Suddenly, a face dangled above me, "Peter!" I screamed in horror. Tears running down my cheeks, settled violently onto my pillow.

"You're okay, Paul. It's me, Miriam, your mother," I heard a voice, calmly say.

I saw a light and heard some chatter in the background, "You did great, son. The surgery was a success," I heard a male voice exclaim. I recognized Mr. Davidson's tone varied with relief and joy dancing together in harmony.

I must have been hallucinating. The accumulation of pain, along with the memories, had subconsciously worked their way into my thoughts; ultimately manifesting them into my dream.

It was far from over though. The horror of my reality might even surpass my nightmares, as I waited to remove the bandages that hid the scars of my life.

Chapter 40

I was still disoriented and feeling sore. It felt like I had just been through a twelve round boxing exhibition with the heavyweight champion of the world. I was accompanied by Mr. Davidson, who remained with me as promised, and my mother, who was still crying.

I heard them mention that Robert had gone into surgery a few hours after I was sedated. Although concerned about Robert, I could not muster up the energy to ask how he was doing. And just as quickly as I had been startled awake, I went back to sleep.

I came out of my slumber to hear Mr. Davidson speaking English with someone. I could not decipher what exactly they were discussing, but it seemed lighthearted and friendly.

"I'm hungry," I said, almost on auto-pilot.

"Okay, what do you want me to get you to eat, son?" Mr. Davidson asked, grabbing the hospital phone to place an order.

"Ice cream sound great or anything sweet would be fine," I replied.

"Hello, can we please have a sample of each one of your desserts and ice creams sent to our room please... yes, this is Mr. Davidson. Thank you very much ma'am," he said, ordering more than required as usual.

I understood that the joy he receives in giving is only multiplied when he is abundantly generous.

I sat silently watching Mr. Davidson jump from one task to another to pacify my mother and I. When it hit me, Mr. Davidson had the soul and innocence of a child. My curiosity had peaked now. I needed to discover why a Christian, who is kindhearted and loving, would belong to a fraternity of *Freemasons,* who supposedly worship the devil.

After a couple of days in recovery, Dr. Santos walked in and explained that I was going to need a month or two of rehabilitation.

Dr. Santos assigned a physical therapist that would assist me in getting more acquainted with my new prosthetics. The physician was extremely kind and helpful. He showed me the advantages of having a prosthetic over a computerized arm. However, I didn't agree.

I was finally released and allowed to return to the Ronald McDonald House. My first day back was also my first session as well. A white van pulled up, in front of the building, with an emblem on the grill and stopped. I wheeled myself out to meet the driver as the aid followed along.

"Hello, son," said the driver, who was coming around the car to help me into the back seat.

"My name is Joe, and I am going to drive you to your rehabilitation sessions for the next month or so," he added, putting on a pair of dark sunglasses and adjusting the mirror.

He was dressed in all white attire and his shirt donned an emblem that read, *Al Malaikah Shriners Transportation*. He also wore a funny looking red hat with a tassel dangling from it. Similar to those wore by Egyptian royalty in the early twentieth century.

"Hello, I am Paul," I timidly said, I was still in the feeling out process. It didn't help that I was unaware why Mr. Davidson was not the one driving me to and from the hospital.

Joe drove towards the hospital, while I studied him closely. Each wrinkle seemed to have a story. He looked about eighty-years-old. He was an extremely distinguished looking old man. His short white hair was receding a bit in the front, with a neatly trimmed beard covering his face. As my inspection moved past his facial features, I noticed the same type of ring on his finger that Mr. Davidson wore every day.

Many thoughts lingered on my mind. A million questions popped up, I wanted to know more about this *brotherhood*.

I knew the road to rehabilitation was not going to be a simple one, but I was prepared to endure many painful and frustrating days on my way to recovery.

The first few days were much of the same. Joe drove me to and from the Shriners Hospital. I was determined to recover much quicker than the doctors projected.

One Friday morning I waited for Joe to arrive as usual and noticed that he was a few minutes late. I was relieved, much due to the fact that I was exhausted and needed a break. Between the physical therapy and English lessons, I rarely had any time to rest my mind.

I almost returned to my room when the Shriners transportation vehicle pulled up to the front and out came Joe with a box of donuts in hand.

"Hope you were not waiting too long for me, son," he said, helping me into the van.

"I thought I would stop and get you some donuts to enjoy. No worries though, you will work it off, I'm sure," he teased, lightening the mood.

"Thank you sir," I answered, amazed at how kind these men were to me.

"I heard from Brother Al that you are doing very well," he said, staring back at me through his rear view mirror with that warm and congenial smile Joe always wore on his face.

"Is Mr. Davidson your brother?" I asked, telling myself, they do not look like brothers.

"Not by birth, but we are brothers," he ambiguously said, all the while maintaining his smile.

I was not sure what that meant, but I was not going to ask him either.

Days turned into weeks. I soon became quite comfortable with Joe. I realized that he was somebodies grandpa, no different than my grandfather back home.

"Thank you sir," I said, as we arrived in front of the Ronald McDonald House.

"It is my duty, my son. By the way, if you ever find yourself in need of anything, just ask one of *us* and we will be there," he replied, helping me out of the vehicle.

Joe wheeled me back inside.

"If you don't mind, I do have a question. When you said, *ask us*, who is *us*?" I asked, mustering up the courage.

"Mr. Davidson did not tell you who *we* are? Why we volunteer? Did he tell you who the Masons are, or about the Shriners Hospitals for Children and how it was founded?" he asked, looking over my shoulder.

He lowered his shades to see my face, he seemed surprised.

"No, he didn't," I answered.

"Do not go anywhere, stay here in the lobby and I will be right back with some pamphlets that will help answer some of your questions," he said, heading out towards the van.

I watched this old man move with such passion and happiness just to answer my questions. This man, someone's grandfather, was a stranger to me, as I was to him, yet treated me like his own. I couldn't point to the reason why I liked him, but I did.

"Okay, son, here is the pamphlet. Take this with you, read it and if you have any questions, do not hesitate to ask me when I see you," Joe said, handing me the pamphlet.

I spent the rest the majority of the evening looking over the pamphlet and surfing the internet for more information regarding Shriners.

The Shriners Hospitals for Children was founded over one hundred years ago by the Freemasons. The mission of the Shriners is to provide help to those children around the world who are suffering with afflictions, such as: orthopedic conditions, burn reconstruction, cleft lip and palate, all free of charge to the patient and the family.

The pamphlet, coupled with the information I discovered online, was enlightening to say the least. However, it left many questions still unanswered... who really are these Freemasons?

I spent much of the night tossing and turning, unable to rest my mind. I was intrigued to learn more about these men who donate their time and money to strangers.

Many of them seemed well-off, and had no personal benefit from volunteering, no reason to give as they did. My grandfather always taught us to *only* take care of our own, yet these men treat strangers, no matter race or religion, as their own.

I woke up with a little more enthusiasm than usual this particular morning knowing that I would ask so many questions in hope that I would uncover the answers.

As always, I waited in the lobby for Joe to pull up. I worked up the nerve and prepped myself mentally to ask the questions, which just last night, seemed so vividly clear.

With each waiting minute, my confidence faded. Reasons not to ask began to outnumber the reasons to ask. There is a quote from book of *Psalms*; *fear not what man can do unto you,* and at this point in my life... I was afraid of no man.

No sooner than I finished my thoughts did the Shriners van pull alongside the curb. A second later, Joe emerged with his white attire and from a distance could be mistaken for an angel.

"Good morning, son. Are you ready to meet the day?" Joe asked.

"Good morning sir," I replied, reciting the questions in my head, one last time, before I asked him, "I am ready to meet the day," I confirmed, as Joe wheeled me to the van and helped me inside.

"How was the pamphlet I gave you?" he asked, buckling his seat belt and adjusting his mirrors before pulling off towards the *east.*

This was it, the reason I tossed and turned all night. I was not going to allow this opportunity to pass me by. My grandpa always reminded us, *ask and you shall receive.*

"Sir, I did find helpful information on the Shriners Hospitals and their mission to be great. However, I could not find much that helped answer a more important question, who are the *Freemasons*?" I replied and awaited his answer.

Joe looked back at me through the rear view mirror and smiled. He lowered his shades so that we made eye contact and with a warmth and confidence nodded.

"That is not a surprising question. I thought you had some life-changing mystery to uncover," he joked. "Son, the answer is simple. Freemasons are men who are a part of the oldest fraternity in the world. We have come together to do our fair share to mend the world we live in. Improve the lives of our families, friends, and finally... ourselves."

Joe's answer was exactly what I witnessed during my short stay and brief encounters with so-called *Mason* men. But I had more questions, there was still an emptiness that lingered in my mind; I wanted to know more.

"What do you have to do in order to be a *Freemason*?" I asked, my comfort level growing and along with it, my curiosity.

"Well son, you must have a desire to help improve yourself, your community, and your country. You must innately want to volunteer and assist others, without being asked. You must live your life, with honor and integrity. But the simple answer is, *to be a Freemason, you must ask one,*" he said, enjoying the conversation as much as I did.

"Do you believe in God?" I asked, with the reservation.

"Yes, all Freemasons must believe in a supreme being. For example, if you are an Atheist, you cannot be an accepted Freemason. However, it doesn't matter if you believe in Islam, Judaism, Christianity, or if you're Buddhists. As long as you believe in the Great Architect of the Universe," he replied, with conviction in his tone.

I hesitated to reveal that I read online that all Freemasons are devil worshipers. And that they believe in Lucifer and commit satanic rituals. Not a conversation I was too comfortable starting with a man I had grown to respect and could be anyone's grandfather. But, as always, I threw caution to the wind...

Chapter 41

"Are Freemasons, Devil worshippers?" I blurted, and then remained silent.

"You read that online somewhere, I assume," he replied, glancing back at me, again, through the rear view mirror. Only this time, he lowered his sunglasses and I got a good look into his piercing blue eyes.

"Yes, I read somewhere that Freemasons worship Lucifer, have satanic rituals, and stuff like that," I continued, as honest as I can be with this kind looking old man.

"Let me teach you something, son. Believe nothing that you hear and only half of what you see. Because, in life, half-truths are more readily available than the truth," he quipped, with a smile.

He displayed his wisdom. An insight reserved only for

men with the time invested in life as he had.

"Lucifer means the Morning Star or the Light Bringer. It is a word of Latin origin and has nothing to do with Satan, my son – absolutely nothing," he added, all the while maintaining that grandfatherly smile that was as warm as the summer's sun.

I began understanding the concept and wisdom that these *Freemasons* shared.

He continued, "The belief that we, Freemasons, share, is the pledge to help improve mankind by any means. And the idea of being *enlightened* is to inform your fellow man and lend a hand to those in need."

Joe seemed like a very kind man. I felt guilty raising the topic.

"Do I look like a devil worshiper to you?" he asked, looking more like Santa Claus than Satan.

"Here I am, at my old age, donating my time, what precious moments left of it, driving you children around. I could spend these final few years of my life with *my* family and grandchildren. But, instead, I am a believer, and will be, to the day I'm buried, that *giving is better than receiving,*" he said, carrying a certain amount of honor and integrity.

He looked back at me again, this time over his shoulder with a warm and gentle smile that put my mind and heart at ease. These *Freemasons*, regardless of the public's perception, seem like great and noble men.

I felt even worse for asking a man, bearing a cross on his neck, a man that could be my grandfather, if he worships the Devil. Who am I to question his belief or to assume such ignorant assumptions?

"Do you attend church, sir?" I asked.

"Please, call me Joe," he kindly requested. "And of course I do, every Sunday, with my family. Part of being a good Mason man is being a good Christian man first."

I wanted to change the mood and lighten the subject with Joe. I felt, I had hurt his feelings with my stupid *Devil* question. I noticed his ring had the letter *G* on it, with some engravings that I couldn't make out.

"I really like your ring, Joe. What does the *G* mean?" I asked, leaning forward to get a closer look.

He pointed to his ring and glanced back at me, "This, *G*, alludes to geometry, the fifth science."

I was a bit confused, "Not sure what that means."

"It translates to the Great Architect of the Universe... God. It is believed that *Geometry* is *God* in thought form. This might be too much for you to understand at once, should I continue my son?" he asked.

"Yes, I am following you," I answered, my curiosity, now, at an all-time high.

He anticipated my next question, "Have you noticed the square and compass on the ring as well?" offering it, for me, to examine.

I stared at this ring, displaying the letter *G*, square, and a compass, and wondered; *what is the symbolism behind it all?*

"Let me explain to you what the square and compass represents," Joe added, keeping his eyes on the road and towards our destination, "The square stands for virtue, my son, a belief that should guide you in all trades with your fellow man or, as we call it; *acting upon the square*. Those who deal otherwise, figuratively speaking, live in the dark."

"What about the compass..." I asked.

"Cannot have one without the other; let me explain. The circle, one draws, with the compass, ties friendship, mortality, and brotherly love knows no beginning and has no end," he said, with honor and reverence.

"Is Mr. Davidson a *Freemason* as well?" I asked, already possessing the truth, but I welcomed the confirmation.

"Yes, Brother Al is a Freemason as well," he answered, while again, staring back at me through the rear view mirror, only this time with a bit of a smile.

"Is he a *Shriner* too?" I questioned.

He added, with pride in his brethren, "Yes, he is. He also is a Hiram Award recipient."

"What is the Hiram Award?" I asked, not sure if that was an English word or Hebrew.

"Hiram award recipients are individuals like Brother Davidson, who have given their time, expertise, and have served their fellow man, selfishly, for many years. It is the highest award that can be bestowed upon a Brother Mason and he has been recognized as such," he said, smiling with pride and joy, as if he was the one receiving the praise that goes along with being recognized.

My views had changed about these *Freemasons*. I

contemplated whether or not I want to be one someday as well. My mother would be *thrilled* to know I'm interest in Freemasonry, since it was she that told me, Freemasons were against *God*. Great, that's all she'd need, her son... part of a cult.

Unfortunately, my parents, my entire village for that matter, were ignorant and uneducated as to what the *Freemasons* were all about.

I spent the next few weeks, with Joe, going to and from the Shriners Hospitals for my rehab, English lessons, and back to the Ronald McDonald House.

My relationship with these men had become a bond of sorts. I prepared two surprises for Mr. Davidson; one was the fact that I wanted to become a Freemason one day. The other surprise was showing Mr. Davidson how well I use my prosthetics. I was going to stand up, on my own, and walk again. Then, with my right hand, give him a gift, as he had given me.

It was a significant moment in my life. The last time I walked, on my own, was that fateful day on Easter Sunday. I presumed he'd appreciate the symbolism as well. It was my resurrection of sorts – my rebirth!

I was eager to showcase my skills to everyone. It was still a bit early and Mr. Davidson had not arrived yet. I wasn't sure he'd visit today. However, typically, he spent his Wednesday's with the children. Mr. Davidson was a CPA, a busy one at that, but still managed to spend as much free time with my brother and me.

I was anxious to show someone my progress. I decided to surprise Jaime, since I had not seen her for the past few days. In addition, I wanted to show her how inspired I was by her positive way of thinking.

I walked out of the room, on my own, and with my new prosthetic... off I went. I headed towards the exit, when a staff member came running towards me.

"Where are you headed, young man," she asked, with a curious look on her face.

"I want to visit my friend who lives across the street," I replied, hoping she understood my broken English and heavy accent.

She knelt down next to me, "Oh, you have a friend, at the Children's hospital, next door?"

"Yes, next door, her name is Jaime and she is my friend," I repeated, pasting my words together with the best of my ability.

"Very well, I will accompany you across the street, if you do not mind, of course," she replied, escorting me across the street.

We entered the lobby and made our way to the front desk, "Jaime, room eight, please," I said.

I imagined the surprise on Jaime's face when I'd show her my new arm, legs, and what I had learned. I was confident that her reaction would be a lot more exaggerated than usual. Still, it was more than welcomed by me.

We reached the room and noticed a woman cleaning up. The staff aid, who accompanied me, spoke to the mysterious lady who resembled Jaime a bit. I wondered if that was Jaime's mother.

"Where is Jaime?" I asked, interrupting the lady gathering items from the drawers.

"I am sorry young man, she is not here anymore," she replied, tears streaming down her face, "Jaime was called home last night."

"I don't understand... where is Jaime?" I repeated, struggling to understand.

"Paul, Jaime died last night from complications due to Leukemia," The staff member explained, with a somber tone.

My heart plummeted deep into my stomach. The veil of invincibility, I felt, moments earlier, had been lifted with a single sentence. I turned around, before the staff aid could help, and walked away.

I was confused. I did not truly know this girl. But, I believed, we had formed a bond. As I crossed the street, with the staff aid behind me, I stopped. I was numb, speechless, and my mind raced in a state of disarray

"Are you okay?" asked the staff aide.

I nodded, "Yes," but I wasn't.

Jaime preached about enjoying life. She insisted on living with courage and happiness, all the while knowing her fate had been all but sealed.

Yet, there I was, whining about my injury, which was only of the flesh. As for Jaime, there was no prosthetic for her affliction. No computerized, plastic, or other limb to repair her ailment.

I reached my room, shoved my face into my pillow, and felt sorry for Jaime. My thoughts then turned to *God*, only this time, it wasn't hostile. Jaime was dying long before we met. Even though I wasn't responsible for her fate, there was a lesson to be learned.

She was sent into my life for a purpose. Some individuals might look perfectly normal on the outside, but on the inside, have suffered irreparable damages.

She taught me to appreciate and embrace your loved ones while you have them. My thoughts quickly turned to Mr. Davidson. I worried about how I treated this man.

I was paralyzed with guilt at the way I addressed Mr. Davidson in the lobby. All he ever wanted to do was help me. I grew up in a household, like many of my friends did, where displaying love and affection was a stranger – a hostile one at that.

Yet this man, this *Christian*, this *Freemason*, this *Shriner*, has been my guardian angel, all along, and I didn't recognize it. I was determined to make amends... before it was too late.

Chapter 42

The following day, I found Mr. Davidson standing around with a few Shriner staff members and some children.

Mr. Davidson noticed me standing on my own. Without a word spoken, we both walked towards each other and embraced. I wanted to say so much but nothing came out. I just held him as he held me. We shared a moment that would stand the test of time.

"This is the happiest day of my life," I managed to whisper. "I will do whatever you ask me to do. You are like my father to me. I owe you my life for what you have done for me and my brother – *I love you.*"

Mr. Davidson struggled to regain his composure as tears now drenched his shirt, he nodded, "Paul, I want you to come with us to church this Sunday."

"*Church*," I asked, "You want me to go to church?"

"Yes, I think we should go together this Sunday," he suggested, his demeanor now a bit more serious, sensing my discontent on the topic.

Before I replied, I stood still, simmered in anger and frustration. I was here, with prosthetic because of church. Now, I'm going return to the place that was responsible for ruining my life and taking my father's youngest son?

"No, I am not interested in church," I snapped, looking down at my artificial feet.

Before I grew any angrier, Jaime's memory immediately reminded me of my earlier intention. I settled myself down a bit, avoiding the same error I was guilty of before.

"Paul, it would make me happy if you came with us," he added, smiling at me with an innocence reserved for children.

I struggled with my feelings on the topic. How was I going to return to the scene of the crime? Essentially, I'd be returning to my *Ground Zero*.

"Please, do me one favor and join us," he insisted.

"Yes," my mother chimed in, "We should go together," tears filled her brown eyes.

I caved, "Fine… fine, I will go with you."

I felt ashamed of myself, as if I had disgraced Peter's memory by agreeing to attend that unholy house of lies.

Mr. Davidson smiled and nodded his head, "Thank you, Paul. You showed me the respect I knew you always possessed."

He was right. It was my way of apologizing for the selfish behavior I displayed in the lobby last month. It was my way of showing him the gratitude and respect he deserved.

As the days passed by, I grew terribly anxious about my unwanted reunion. I was afraid of how I'd react on Sunday. Being raised a Christian, church was *God's* home, and, in my opinion, *he* was directly responsible for my affliction.

I spent the final days leading up to mass, polishing up my English. I learned the mannerisms and phrases that would allow me to properly communicate with other folks who spoke the language.

I eagerly attended my classes and reminisced about Jaime's spirit. Although I only knew her for an extremely brief period of time, she affected me a great deal with her courage, passion, and zest for life.

I spent the Saturday night resting in my bed, preserving my energy for my big confrontation with *God* in the morning. My thoughts tossed me around like a helpless boat, caught, in the *perfect storm*. I prepared to confront the knock that would soon be at my door.

With church weighing heavily on my mind, my thoughts turned to the aftermath of my American Voyage. What was I to do when I returned back home? Compared to the United States, my homeland seemed primitive and a dead-end at best.

I gained valuable knowledge on computers. However, in my country, how much demand was there for my skill? We were farmers, needing farm hands, physical labor, and with my situation, I was useless. I faced a more daunting issue, as I accepted that my future back home seemed bleak at best.

I opened my laptop and began feverishly searching alternatives. Only this time, I erased my browser history to ensure that my plan would remain *top secret*.

"Wake up, we're going to be late," my mother shouted, pulling the covers off Robert.

I sat up, "When is Uncle Al going to arrive?"

My mother smiled, "Uncle Al?"

I didn't reply, I just smirked and got ready.

"Good," she exclaimed, "You should have called him that since we arrived."

I hardly objected, since it was true. Mr. Davidson, *Uncle Al*, had earned that title.

Uncle Al arrived early as usual. If he was anything, he was precise. He wanted to reach the church before anyone else. His motto was: *be the host, not the guest.*

Placing the bag of sweets down, he cheered, "Good morning, good morning... everyone, good morning!"

As we grew closer to our final destination, I grew more anxious. The butterflies ordinarily associated with this feeling had transformed into dragons, slashing their way through my stomach.

I sat in front, per Uncle Al's request, and noticed a cross in the distance. It seemed alive, growing larger with each waning moment. We finally reached the church and pulled around back. Everyone got out of the car but me.

I gathered myself, took a deep breathe, and opened

the door. Uncle Al stayed waited behind to support me. That was just his nature.

I got out and followed closely behind. I was caught in a bitter struggle. I battled the haunting memories of that macabre Easter Sunday afternoon. With each step forward, I returned to the site where I lost everything.

The smell the church incense creeping under my skin. I felt vulnerable and cold. I shivered a bit. My body tensed up in fear.

Uncle Al reached the top of the stairway, before asking, "Are you okay?"

I stared ahead, almost in a trance. I was numb, my body felt weak, and my mind was terrified of what lay ahead.

Yet, with two words, "I am," we moved forward to face my demons. Only this time, I was not alone. He opened the church door and a rush of air followed.

I surveyed the entrance and walked past a set of candles. I turned the corner to move along when I was confronted by the object of my hate. I feeling of panic ravaged my body, leaving me dizzy and weak.

I confronted the gigantic idol of Jesus Christ that adorned the church hallway. I stared in horror as I investigated every small detail that this sculpture possessed. From the dried up wax tears, the blood dripping from a crown of thorns, his head titled sideways in submission, while his hands and feet brutally impaled by years of sin and betrayal.

Tears stormed from my eyes, without permission, and

without mercy. I tried concealing my condition from Uncle Al, but it was far too late.

He put his arm around me, sharing my tears and my pain. I whimpered silently, before a cry pierced my soul and tore through my body. I collapsed to the floor while Uncle Al knelt beside me.

It was a moment of peace, my time of forgiveness, and Uncle Al shared my awakening. I knew, in my heart and soul, the only medicine would remedy my pain was returning to my heavenly father.

A few minutes passed by and so did onlookers, "Is he okay?" asked a woman dressed in black.

Uncle Al nodded, "Yes, he is okay now."

I was at the mercy of my emotions. The anger and frustration had built up inside me like a ticking time bomb. Luckily for me, it was defused before an explosion, or even worse, an implosion that would have caused irreversible damage to what remained of my soul.

I finally gathered the courage to look up at onlookers, at Uncle Al as well, who reassured me to stand up and face my fears... the future. No amount of surgery or prosthetics would mend my wounds. The healing process required a rebirth of sorts and returning to the scene of the crime was the only remedy.

Uncle Al escorted me into the church auditorium and into a sea of people who had earlier witnessed our incident. We reached the middle seats but were encouraged to sit up front.

The Priest approached us, "In the name of the Father,

the Son, and the Holy Spirit," he repeated the prayer a few times. At this point, everyone wept, including Uncle Al.

Towards the conclusion of the sermon, the priest encouraged us to gather around and take pictures.

Uncle Al offered me a large hand-carved crucifix, "Are you up for it?"

I nodded, "Yes."

I was finally ready to forgive. I was prepared to move on and live my life. I had not died in that blast, but merely knocked down and wounded.

I needed to pick myself up, brush myself off, and care to my wounds; but live! This was for Peter, for Robert, for Jaime, *and* to show those animals that they couldn't kill me, or my spirit. But most of all, I had to live... for myself.

Chapter 43

*T*he car ride back was quiet, allowing everyone to think. Words weren't necessary. Our actions had spoken volumes. We sat in comfortable silence, all the way back to the Ronald McDonald House where we ended the evening alone.

The following morning, I heard the phone ring, "Okay, we'll start preparing," my mother replied.

"Who was that?" I asked.

"That was Dr. Santos. He informed me that your rehabilitation has been far more successful than imagined and there is no reason to stay here anymore. Plus, our Visa is about to expire again," she added.

My heart raced. I did not want to go back to that country. I had nothing to look forward to. I had, in a sense, outgrown my own backyard – overstayed my welcome. It was time for me to move on, build a life for myself, a future not restricted to farming or hard labor.

I decided to change my destination. It was then, that I devised my plan, unbeknownst to anyone else. I grabbed my laptop and began planning my escape. I knew it required the utmost secrecy, understanding just how perceptive Uncle Al was.

I checked my funds to confirm I had enough. It was, of course, the money I received from Uncle Al that would allow my family to get home. Only I wasn't returning home. I had a new place in mind. A land I briefly visited once.

Though we didn't require any further rehabilitation, I did continue attending English class. The ability to speak English was vital for me, maybe more than ever.

If I were to pull off any type of espionage, communication would play a major role. I knew it would probably take a bit more than that. However, I wasn't going back to the land of the dead. And that was all the motivation I needed.

I prepared everything I needed to pull this stunt off the night before my escape. I verified the costs, checked the flight, and contemplated where to stay. I had enough money to keep me afloat for a few days. But, not enough to get a room for more than a night, maybe two, depending on how run-down the motel was. Then again, I wasn't checking in to the Waldorf Astoria. Plus, a hotel couldn't be any safer than the church where I lost my limbs.

I felt terribly sick, my stomach twisted and turned. My intestines almost wrestled their way out through my throat.

"Are you okay, son?" my mother asked, staring at me from under her eyebrows.

"Yes... yes, I am okay," I replied, believing that if my dear mother uncovered my plan, Uncle Al was soon to follow.

"You are acting strange," she added.

"We're leaving in the morning. I spoke to Uncle Al and he cannot escort us to the airport. He is busy with a client. But, he promised to try and cancel his appointment for us," I said.

"No, tell him not to cancel," she replied, "Never mind, I will call him myself."

I grabbed the phone from my mother's hand, "I will take care of it."

My mother completely understood. While being the gentle hearted, trusting, and sometimes naïve person, she was, she believed my story.

I felt terribly guilty for not thanking Uncle Al for all the wonderful things he had done for me and my family. Leaving without a goodbye was a terrible decision, borderline betrayal, and it began eating at my conscience.

I considered calling him to say goodbye. Nothing more, a simple farewell would suffice. However, I knew he'd have a million questions. I wouldn't be surprised if he showed up to drive us to the airport. Actually, I'd be surprised if he didn't. My only saving grace was that our tickets still indicated a return trip to Iraq and there was no way of changing that – none that I knew.

Luckily, I found a loop hole, so to speak, a small window of opportunity that I would manipulate to my advantage. I just couldn't leave without saying goodbye. Though, I knew that was not something I can do over the phone. He was too caring and always wanted to help. A generic adios wouldn't suffice and I was most aware of that fact.

I called his cell phone, but was transferred directly to his voice mail recording, "Uncle Al, please call me back immediately. I have something extremely important to tell you," I ended the call and waited.

Twenty minutes had passed with no response. I became desperate, almost panicked, as the window of opportunity was closing. I paced back and forth only causing my mother more stress than she already carried.

"What is wrong, Paul. Tell me, please, you're worrying me. Is everything okay?" she pled, concerned like any mother would be.

"Everything is fine, mother, I am just nervous about going back home... that's all," I lied, avoiding eye contact. I was too smart to fool around with my mother's intuition.

I could not wait any longer, I quickly re-dialed Uncle Al's phone and received nothing but his voice mail once again. I hung up and repeated dialing him over and over until he finally answered.

"What is it Paul? I am at a play with my wife and daughter," Uncle Al whispered.

"I need to see you tonight," I answered, trying to conceal the panic in my voice that would have been apparent to anyone.

"What is wrong? Tell me, because I cannot just get up and leave, Paul," he insisted.

"No, I need you now, right now. This cannot be discussed over the phone and it cannot wait either. Uncle Al, I must see you within the hour, I am running out of time," I begged, my panic turned into desperation and I began doubting my plan.

I heard a woman's voice pleading for Uncle Al to get off the phone, "I cannot do this right now, I am sorry, Paul. I am with my family and I will call you when this play is over," he replied.

"No, please. Come now. Hello...hello?" I realized the call had been ended.

I sat silently, not even a thought lived in my head. I was numb, afraid, and felt alone again. My confidence, in my plan, ended with that call. What seemed like a sure thing, a bullet proof plan, had now turned into a terrible disaster just waiting to happen.

I advised my mother to finish packing what was left and be prepared to leave. I called the cab company, instead of using the drivers they provided to avoid peaking suspicion from the staff.

We waited anxiously for the cab driver to notify us that they've arrived. Uncle Al never left my mind. I now know there are individuals that bestow miracles upon total strangers; they're called *Shriners*.

I was going to betray Uncle Al's trust and abandon him without as much as a goodbye.

As time dragged along, the phone rang, "Mom, can you get that. It's the cab company," I told her.

"Hello... oh, hi, Al," my mother answered.

I quickly took the phone from her, "Uncle Al?" I asked, confirming it was him.

"Yes, Paul, I decided to leave the play and come visit you. Where are you? And what is the problem?" he asked. I recognized a bit of frustration and even annoyance in his tone.

"I am at the Ronald McDonald room. Please come here and then we can talk," I insisted.

"Okay, I will be there in fifteen minutes," he replied, ending the call without saying goodbye.

I knew he was angry or, at the very least, irritated with the situation. I don't blame him one bit. This imposing demand would have caused Mother Teresa to lose her patience – possibly her temper.

Chapter 44

Our layover stop, before Iraq, was Frankfurt, Germany, and it was in on that stop I'd make my escape. I was not sure where I'd go or what I'd. However, I was sure that my motherland was no longer an option.

I waited for what felt like hours. Finally, a knock on the door and in walked Uncle Al.

"What is it?" he asked, concerned and irritated.

"I am leaving... I am flying in less than four hours," I replied, struggling to make eye contact.

"Leaving? Where are you going?" he asked, shocked and puzzled to hear my confession.

"We are flying back home, well, my mother will be," I answered in English, concealing the fact from my dear mother who was still in the dark.

"Let us talk outside for a moment, Paul," Uncle Al requested.

"What is going on? Tell me the truth," he demanded.

I stared at him for a moment. I realized that nothing less than the absolute truth would suffice. He was too intuitive to fool and more importantly, he deserved the truth.

"I am not going back home, I am going to abandon my flight when we land in Frankfurt," I answered.

"I didn't know you were leaving to Iraq, let alone to Germany. When did this happen, when did you decide this... how did you buy tickets?" he rattled off, in succession.

"I have been thinking about my future since the operation. Add Jaime's death and the incident at church it was then, on that day, I decided to take back my life. I'm sorry I didn't tell you earlier. I just couldn't face you. But, I could not leave without at least saying goodbye," I confessed.

"What are you going to do in Germany? Where will you live? *How* will you live? How much money do you have remaining after buying your tickets? Have you thought any of this through?" he continued, "This is absurd, you don't just up and decide to defect into another country, and it isn't that easy. They will discover where you are from and send you packing – sooner or later."

"Tell me how to do this, I need your help. But, I have decided, with our without your help, I am not going back to a dead end life," I insisted, feeling discouraged after listening to a sobering reality.

Uncle Al stared at me for a moment and shook his head. He placed his hand on my shoulder and we walked back in together.

"I will make some phone calls and we will figure this out together. I don't agree with what you are doing, but I won't allow you to fail in doing so," he said, flashing a smile that can encourage even the most disheartened of men, "I'll be right back."

After only five minutes, Uncle Al re-entered the room and pulled me aside, "Here is an additional *two-thousand dollars*, which is all that I have with me in cash and all I can get my hands on at this hour. That should suffice for a while. Regardless, I'll stay in contact as much as possible once you have made it through the terminal in Frankfurt," he continued.

We sat down together and I heard his plan, "When you land in Frankfurt, I want you to destroy and discard all of your identification – everything. You will seek refuge asylum but you will not keep any information with you. You can use an alias until you leave the airport and into Germany," he explained, with a serious tone.

I leaned forward emphasizing my interest.

"When the plane lands in Frankfurt, you are going to seek refuge in the public men's room. You will remain there until your flight has departed – not a moment sooner. Are we clear?" he asked, staring into my eyes in an attempt to gauge whether or not I was going to be able to pull this off.

"Yes, I got it. I will stay in the Men's room until the

plane has taken off. I will destroy all my identification and choose a fictitious name," I repeated, nodding to display that I understood his plan.

"Once you enter Germany, you will locate a con-venience store, at which time you will purchase a temporary calling card and contact me immediately. I will have further instructions and the ability to wire you additional funds at that time. That should keep you housed until we figure this out completely," he said, searching for any sign of uncertainty.

I wasn't going to give him a single reason to reconsider, not a shadow of a doubt. Although, I wasn't sure what my future had in store for me, I was sure it was better than the grim outcome awaiting me in that primitive land.

"I want you to know, that in the beginning, when I first arrived, I was suspicious. I did not trust you or anyone involved for that matter. I was betrayed, in my opinion, by *God,* and I wasn't going to be fooled again," I admitted, "But, as time has gone by, I had the opportunity to know you better. I've come to acknowledge, that you are a man of your word, a man of honor, and integrity. You are a good man, a Christian man, a *Freemason.*"

"You don't have to explain, my son, I..." he tried replying.

But I had to express my gratitude and the fact that I looked at him as a mentor, "You must know how I feel about you Uncle Al. I was so adamant in showing you how much I didn't trust you, so at the very least, I can show you the opposite," I added, feeling the need to open up to this man.

Uncle Al's tears were now streaming, "Please, stop, please, you are embarrassing me."

I ignored his requests, "You have shown me how I should live my life. By example, you have given me an idea of what a man of honor and integrity resembles. I will carry the lessons I've learned from you, for the rest of my life. You have given me a second chance at happiness. Another shot at something I thought was all but lost. I promise you, I will not squander this chance."

Uncle Al nodded, "I know you will, son."

I wasn't done, "I will live this life as a gift, a blessing, and I will make you proud that you have invested in me so sincerely. I want to grow up to be a man of honor and integrity. I want to become a man of justice, charity, compassion. I will grow up and be like you, Uncle Al, a *Freemason* man," I said, looking up to see his reaction at my disclosure, my confession – my desires.

Uncle Al's patted my shoulder, "Son, I have only done what is incumbent of me. I live by no other creed other than to serve my fellow man. I believe in doing what is righteous, honorable, and I hope you will do the same in your life," he advised, fighting back tears.

I hugged him and cried, "You have saved my life."

We embraced for a moment... maybe our last together.

"Okay, so let's figure this out. When you land in Frankfurt, you are going to discard all of your identification and remain in the men's room until you are absolutely positive the plane has departed," he repeated himself.

We spent the next few minutes just sitting around talking, sharing laughs, and memories. Before we knew it, the time had arrived to head towards the airport. We all piled in his luxury sedan and made our way to LAX.

We arrived around 4:30 am. Uncle Al stopped in the visitor's parking lot and we made our way towards the terminal. My paranoia peaked, as I wondered, what happens if I get caught? My mind raced from one nightmare scenario to another.

"Let's stand near the security gate to ensure we make it through on time," Uncle Al gestured towards the flight screen indicating Frankfurt as a layover. Nonetheless, to some, it was a final destination.

"Stay in touch with me my, son," Uncle Al cried.

We embraced again and said our goodbyes. I didn't know if this was the last time I'd ever see this man, my friend, and mentor – ever again.

"I will Uncle Al, I will see you again," I said, hoping this was not a goodbye, but simply, *until next time.*

As we reached the gates, Robert and my mother both passed the security clearance. I followed closely behind. I reached for my identification, ticket, and passport and presented them to the security officer.

He looked at me with suspicion, or at least I thought he did, "Sir, please step out of the line and move over to the security booth for further evaluation."

It can't be, I thought to myself, "What is wrong?"

"Just move over to the designated area and wait," he ordered.

This was it. I was caught... but how? I replayed all the mistakes I could have possibly made and I couldn't find a single one.

I was desperate and afraid. I turned to Uncle Al who owned a look of concern and confusion. Only one person could save me from this nightmare, and that was the same person who put me here – *God!*

Chapter 45

"Sir, your visa is expired. You cannot get on this plane until that is corrected," the officer said, in a matter of fact tone.

"What? This must be a mistake. Uncle Al corrected this already, please, check again," I begged, the concern in my voice had now climaxed into panic mode.

Did they know of my plan? I tried to remain calm. I took a deep breath and turned towards Uncle Al who was talking to the officer and on his phone as well.

"Paul, your passport has not been processed as of yet. Remember, this is earlier than you were expected to fly and the passport process has not been completed. Luckily, I have friends who will expedite this process for us. However, it won't be fixed until tomorrow afternoon.

At that time, you'll be back on schedule. I don't know what else to say, son, I'm sorry," Uncle Al explained.

I smiled to comfort him, "Don't be sorry, Uncle Al, this is not your fault. This was, completely, my responsibility. And thank you for fixing it so quickly. I don't' know what I'd do without you."

How was I going to pull this off in Germany? I failed to board the plane leaving the United States... legally.

We grabbed our bags and drove to a motel. Robert and my poor mother were terribly confused and sat silently. We signed out of the Ronald McDonald House and checking back in would be nearly impossible – even with Uncle Al.

We pulled into a parking lot on Ventura Blvd, "This should be fine for the night," he said, "I'll be right back. I'll grab us a room."

I watched him heading to the motel lobby and couldn't help but wonder, what type of a man takes time away from his family and business, to help strangers in the middle of the night.

He returned a few minutes later and gestured for us to follow him to our room for the night. We reached our room, which was located on the second floor of a motel.

I was eager to get my life back on track. Though, I was aware that adjusting back to life, outside the United States, was going to be a bit difficult for me. Either way, I'd cross that bridge when I reached it. For now, one step at a time was the remedy.

We stayed up playing cards and listening to Uncle Al

telling jokes to pass the time away, which, by the way, moved to a crawl. The anticipation of waiting for my passport approval weighed heavily on my mind. I spent half the time paying attention to the activities and the other half staring at the clock.

Approximately a quarter after nine, Uncle Al received a call, "Approved!" somehow or another, he managed to get my passport status and visa approved. We contacted the airlines and rescheduled the flight as standby.

They accommodated our request much sooner than expected. We weren't expecting to correct the problem this quickly. Nonetheless, I was elated and anxious to try this again, this time hoping for a clearance at check-in.

We returned to the airport and began the process again. My mother and Robert moved in front of me in the security line. I knew they would clear without a problem. I wanted to make sure that I would be the last person they checked in. That way, if there were any questions regarding my passport, they'd be immediately addressed.

I finally reached the TSA agent. My identification and documents were prepared and in hand awaiting to be cleared.

"Good afternoon sir, where are you headed today?" the TSA agent asked, reviewing my identification.

"Germany," I accidently replied.

"Germany? It says here on your ticket you are headed to Iraq," she questioned, puzzled at my response, which must have raised a red flag.

"I mean, I land in Frankfurt first, then to Iraq," I

quickly responded, forcing a smile, while I held it together.

She looked at my tickets a few times, as well as my identification and passport, "Please wait here, I'll be right back," moving towards her desk, near the side of the line, where a desktop computer was sitting.

Although I was nervous, there was nothing to be worried about, I told myself – not yet at least. If I were to pull this off in Frankfurt, I needed to be near perfect. I absolutely couldn't afford to make these types of mistakes, some ten thousand miles away, in a foreign land.

Finally, after a few tense moments of waiting my TSA agent returned, "Here you go," she smiled and gave me back my I.D. and itinerary.

I turned to Uncle Al and waved goodbye. We were both fighting back tears. I wondered when I would see him again, if ever. The thought of being aided by a total stranger, to me, was still mindboggling and hard to fathom. But I was living proof.

I sat nervously awaiting the airline's to announce our boarding. I scanned the passengers who were also sitting in our section. One thing I did have on my side, if I were to pull this off, was that my skin color was lighter than most of the people in my culture. Blending in to German society would be easier on me, because I took my mother's color, than on Robert, who inherited my father's dark complexion.

Finally, the airline representative announced the boarding of our flight. We all stood up and began to file behind one another with our tickets in hand. I reminded myself that I was boarding this plane legally. I knew that in order to pull this off successfully in Frankfurt, I needed to maintain my composure better than I was doing here, in Los Angeles.

"Have a nice flight," said the airline representative.

I boarded the plane behind my family and settled down inside. I found my seat and tried to place my bag in the storage compartment. However, I was unable to keep my balance with my new prosthetics. Luckily, a man who was sitting across from my seat jumped up and helped.

"Where are you headed?" he asked.

"Iraq," I replied, by habit.

I was a wreck. Not only was it hard to pull this stunt off, now I had revealed to the man, sitting directly across from me, that my final destination was Iraq. How was I going to merge, unnoticed, with those who were destined in Frankfurt without arousing suspicion from this passenger?

We were instructed on the flight regulations and procedures. Within a few minutes, after the captain's instructions, we were off and flying.

I recalled how I was just on a plane heading to the City of Angels to repair my damaged and uncertain future. When hope and my faith were all but lost, an angel, Al Davidson, salvaged what was left of my miserable existence.

I continually reminded myself just how hopeless I felt a few months earlier, in that Baghdad hospital. I had made tremendous progress against all hopes and expectations.

Yet, I couldn't help but feel terribly nervous as that haunting cloud of doubt crept in undetected and crashed violently above my head. I wasn't destined for happiness. This wasn't going to end well – I knew no other truth.

Chapter 46

R obert and my mother were absolutely oblivious to my plans. I actually had changed my mind, mid-flight, and decided to take my brother with me to Frankfurt. He was my twin, my only surviving sibling. I planned to leave my mother aboard the flight, and head home, to my father, as scheduled.

As much as Robert's presence would hinder me, I had failed my dear brother Peter, and I couldn't bear to live with the guilt of letting Robert down as well.

My mother, on the other hand, was better off back home. My father would have given chase anyway, complicating my entire plan had she not come through those gates at Baghdad International.

I had my plan all thought out by now and ready to be implemented. I couldn't get myself to sleep on the flight, even though I was extremely tired. The twelve or so hour flight felt more like twenty-four hours. Plus, my mind wouldn't allow a moment of rest; my nerves were rattled as I anticipated the next phase of my plan.

I lay my head against the window staring out into the, now, familiar sea of clouds that accompanied us silently throughout the flight. My heart slowed to a rhythmic pace, accepting the events that were soon to follow.

I was startled by the shuffling of passengers all around me. The captain had begun announcing our arrival in Germany within forty-five minutes.

My heart pounded inside my chest. I felt it beat and almost heard it as well. My palms filled with cold sweat as my stomach twisted and wrestled with itself. It was too much to endure, too much for one teenage boy, who already suffered a lifetime's worth of pain and anguish – too much for anyone.

I replayed the process in my mind. The airplane violently met the runway, shaking all aboard as if to announce our arrival. The difference between those who succeeded and those who failed was contingent upon one trait and one *trait* only... preparation – I was prepared.

Now, I needed to convince my brother to follow along without questioning me. I raced up front and found my brother sitting silently listening to his music. I whispered to him from the seat behind, but he seemed to be ignoring me.

I noticed that he had ear plugs on and was most likely the reason for the silence. I nudged his shoulder to get his attention. He turned around he smiled when he saw it was me.

"Come with me Robert. I have to use the bathroom, but I'd rather not get off here alone," I said, as he seemed okay with the idea.

Without a single question asked, Robert stood up, and waited for me to lead.

"Grab your bag from the overhead as well," I added, trying to seem as subtle possible.

"Why do I need my bag, Paul?" he asked, while searching for his bag in the overhead above us.

"Just get it and I'll explain why when we reach the men's room," I replied, as my eyes scanned for that passenger who knew that I was destined for Iraq.

I managed to avoid my mother and blend in with the passengers who were leaving the plane in a single filed line. I avoided eye contact with essentially everyone until we were clear across the terminal and near the men's room. I immediately found an empty stall for the handicapped.

"Why are we here?" he asked.

I placed my finger over my mouth and whispered, "I'll explain in a minute. Just trust me, okay?"

It broke my heart to see my younger brother in this condition. After the explosion, Robert had the mental capacity of a child. In the explosion, my brother and I were never the same. I not only lost Peter and my limbs, but my younger twin lost something he'd never regain... his mind.

I was so inundated with my self-centered views. I

failed to see exactly the damage my brother sustained during that blast. I might have lost my legs and arm, which the doctors were able to replace. However, the doctors were unable to repair my brother's injuries. His affliction had no remedy, no prosthetic, and no cure.

I promised myself that as long as I existed, I'd be my brother's keeper. It was my duty, my solemn vow, to care for him as long as I lived. I had taken this personal oath before, and failed. This time, only my death would derail my pledge.

Chapter 47

As the minutes turned to an hour, many people attempted to open the door and some asked if everything was okay. It was becoming a problem to just simply sit in the stall. I was terrified that airport personnel might check to verify that there was no security breach or danger. It was a realistic possibility that I desperately needed to avoid.

"Stay in here and do *not* open the door for anyone until I come back," I instructed Robert.

I tried checking the time to gauge exactly how long we needed to stay out of sight. But there was no clock in the men's room. I also needed to ensure that my mother had not caught on to the plan and alarmed the police.

I asked him again to confirm that he understood me, "Do not open the door until I come back, do you understand Robert?"

"Yes, I will stay here until you come back, Paul. Please don't leave me here. I don't want to stay here alone," Robert begged, holding my hand.

"Of course not, don't be silly, Robert. I will just check on mom and be right back. Just stay in here and do not open the door until you hear me come back and knock," I repeated, knowing that I had no choice but to quickly run out and verify that my plan had not been foiled.

I unlocked the bathroom stall door and cracked it open just a bit. My view was limited at best. I bent down and peaked under the stalls to spot anyone else who might be in a stall.

Nothing, the bathroom, as far as I can tell was empty at the moment. This was the best opportunity I had to make a quick exit to check the time. I knew what when the layover ended and just how long before the flight would take off.

I hurried outside the bathroom and begin searching for the closest clock. I roamed the terminal before finding a café and realized that our flight departed in less than fifteen minutes.

I hurried back to the men's bathroom to ensure that my brother was safe and, more importantly, where I left him. I found myself turned around a bit and puzzled as to which stall I had left him in.

My heart raced, my palms dripped with sweat, as I reached near panic mode. I hoped I didn't take too long, forcing Robert to come out and blow our cover.

I quickly entered the first men's room I found, called out to Robert, and received no response. I looked under the stalls to find his feet. I quickly checked the end stall that was designated for the handicap and nothing.

I left the bathroom and moved to the remaining men's room. This must be the one I left him in, I told myself. My deepest fear was coming to life with each moment that I couldn't find Robert. My body ached from the pulsating blood running frantically through my fragile veins, which were reattached during surgery.

"Robert, are you in here?" I whispered, entering the final men's room before I'd reach the boarding gate. I bent down and again scanned the stalls for waiting feet and nothing – I had lost him.

I ran out of the men's room and looked around. My face must have been as obvious as my fears. Sweat raced down my forehead and into my eyes. I was terrified and soon, I'd be caught.

Suddenly, an arm grabbed me from behind, "Paul..." said a voice that sounded familiar. I realized it was Robert standing behind me alone and in tears.

"Why did you leave the bathroom? Didn't I make it clear to you to remain there until I returned? I told you to stay, you disobeyed me again!" I snapped, as the fear and relief of finding him safe overwhelmed me for a moment.

"I am sorry Paul, I thought you abandoned me and I was afraid. People were knocking on the door and asking me to come out. I am sorry," Robert cried, the tears slid down his face and dove to the floor below.

"It's fine. Do not cry, Robert. I am sorry I yelled at

you. Everything is okay now," I said, trying to get him to follow me back to the men's room again.

"I'm hungry, can we eat?" Robert asked, pointing to the fast food stand across the hall, which, by the way, was swamped with passengers from our flight earlier.

"Can you wait a few minutes?" I asked.

"I am hungry, Paul. Where is mom?" he replied.

I knew that if his intent was to find our mother, nothing would stop me from changing his mind.

"Fine, let's go grab something to eat and pick up food for mom, she must be hungry as well, don't you think?" I replied, diverting his attention back to food and away from returning to our mother for the moment.

I knew that if I could just delay him, for a few more minutes, the flight would take off and I'd begin the second phase of my plan safely – *If I could...*

Chapter 48

As we stood in line waiting to order from the menu, I noticed a few people staring at us. I became used to the fact that people stared at us and would, for the rest of our lives. However, at this precise moment, I was unable to shake the notion that they were on to my plan.

We received our food, and began moving back to the stall, "I want to sit here and eat," Robert sat down and began eating.

To avoid a scene, I reluctantly agreed and found us a different table. While Robert continued eating, I searched through his bag and removed all of his identification. I placed both of our information in a plastic bag and discarded the bag in the nearest trash can.

I scanned the terminal for any peculiar behavior and

ensuring my mother had not notified the captain. However, it seemed like everyone was now staring at us.

"Are you done, Robert?" I asked, urging him to finish quicker.

But, he refused to change pace. My brother was oblivious to what was happening at this point. Finally, he finished his meal, wrapped up his fork, plate, and stood up. I grabbed his bag and moved directly towards the trash can.

We found an empty stall again, only this time, we'd remained here. I tried entertaining Robert a bit, in an attempt to keep him occupied.

There was a tugging on the handle, "Is anyone in here?" a voice asked, "Hello?"

"Yes, it is being used," I replied, trying to keep Robert quiet.

But, he answered as well, "Yes, we are in here, go away."

I placed my hand over his mouth and gestured for him to remain silent – but it was too late. Not more than five minutes later, I heard a walkie-talkie go off and footsteps approaching the bathroom stall where we were hiding.

I kept my hand on his mouth, "Shh..." I whispered.

"Open the door please. I must make sure everyone is okay in there," Demanded a voice with a German accent and followed by a few knocks on the door. I remained quiet, as the knocking grew louder and more intense. I heard a request for reinforcements to arrive.

My heart thumped and my mouth turned dry. I

struggled to swallow my fears, I was trapped, cornered, and my plan was thwarted. I wasn't sure what to expect if I was caught. Would they throw me in prison? Would they deport us back to the United States or put my brother and me on the next flight back to Northern Iraq? My mind raced at the possibilities, none of which were in my favor.

"Open the door now or I will break it open," a male voice ordered, now angry.

I whispered, in my language, "Not a word. Just stay quiet and allow me to do all the talking."

Robert again nodded in agreement. However, I wasn't sure just exactly how much of my request he understood and more importantly... would follow.

I finally gave up, unlocked the bathroom stall door, and came out.

"Who are you? And why are you both hiding in the bathroom stalls?" the head officer asked me, checking the stall for information or evidence.

"I am sorry, but my brother needed to use the bathroom and he needed my help. My brother is mentally handicapped from an injury and I look after him. I have some disabilities as well," I replied, avoiding too much eye contact with the tall, German officer.

"When is your flight going to take off?" he asked, as they continued searching for more information as to our identity.

"I think we might have missed it officer," I answered, positive that we had missed our flight, just like I planned.

"We're going to get you on the next flight available and you will wait on stand-by at your terminal," he ordered, escorting us back to our terminal.

I nodded, "Thank you."

"Stay here and wait for the next opening. And do not miss that flight. Do you understand me, son?" asked the officer, leaning forward to emphasize his request.

"Yes, we will wait here and board the next flight sir," I replied, pretending to be an astute and obedient young man.

As the officers scattered around the terminal and throughout the airport, I knew that my opportunity to escape and blend in with German civilians was narrowing quickly. I prepared to make my move soon, knowing there was absolutely no room for error.

Five minutes had passed before I grabbed Robert by the arm and made a mad dash towards the exit. As we turned the final corner, I saw daylight shining through only a few hundred feet ahead, as well as a final security guard who seemed to have locked eyes with me.

I turned away, continued towards the exit, and didn't look back to see if the officer was in pursuit. I threw all caution to the wind and took my chance at a new beginning.

We reached the exit and were on German land within a minute of our attempt. We continued down the road and blended in with German citizens.

"We made it," I whispered.

Robert asked, "Did I make it, too?"

I turned my face and began crying. I made sure that Robert did not see my tears. I was now, officially, a guest of this land, a foreigner to this unfriendly world – a stranger in the crowd.

Chapter 49

After walking at a frantic pace for at least twenty minutes, I felt safe enough to rest at a park nearby. We sat down, or at least I sat down, for a moment to gain my composure and capture my breath. Robert fed the pigeons sunflower seeds that he had stuffed in his pocket.

I smiled as the tears ran down my face, crashing to the hard and unforgiving land beneath my feet. My dear mother had no idea, and in all likelihood, terribly worried that her two boys are missing, helplessly abandoned and alone.

After briefly resting, I knew the sun was to set soon and I desperately needed to secure a place to sleep for the night. I still had approximately two-thousand dollars remaining with me. However, it was all that we had in a land where I didn't speak the language, nor knew a friendly face.

Robert complained about resting and being hungry again, but I continued searching for a familiar shop to find a person with something in common.

Around the corner, I spotted a coffee shop. It looked like an internet café of sorts. I immediately grabbed Robert by the arm and crossed the street.

As we entered, I turned to Robert, "Have a seat and wait for me here."

"Grab me a cake, Paul," he asked.

I nodded, "Just sit down."

The lady behind the counter greeted me in German, "Wie kann ich Ihnen helfen?"

"Hi, I don't speak the language, I'm sorry. I do speak English though," I replied, hoping she spoke English as well.

"Yes, American, you are welcome here. What do you like?" she asked, smiling.

"Can I have an orange juice and two slices of the German pound cake, please? Also, where are your rest rooms?" I asked, reaching into my pocket to pay for my order.

"Coming right up," she said, "The men's room is to your left and around the corner."

She thoroughly inspected my money before giving me back my change, but, not in U.S. currency, in Euro.

"Follow me," I ordered Robert.

I stared in the mirror and smiled. I was relieved that I made it. I was free from the dead-end life back home and had a chance at a fresh start. We cleaned up and went back out to our seat.

I didn't realize that our order had been waiting for us the entire time, "Excuse me, your juice and cake is here," the lady behind the counter said, pointing to our order.

"Thank you," I replied.

As I grabbed my order, I noticed a flyer advertising a Middle-Eastern restaurant on the counter named *Habibi*.

"Where is this place?" I asked.

She pointed straight behind me, "It is about a mile down the road and around the corner."

"Thank you, again," I replied.

"Get up, Robert, we can walk and eat," I implored, putting my jacket back on to leave.

"I want to sit and finish my cake before we leave, Paul," Robert answered, stubbornly sitting and ignoring my request.

"We can walk and eat. It will be dusk soon and we have no place to stay," I insisted, holding back my anger.

"I want to see mom. Why are we not with mom? Why are we here? Where are we?" he asked, in succession.

"We will see mom later, Robert. And this *is* our new home," I sternly replied, grabbing his arm and helping him up to his feet.

We left the café and headed towards the restaurant. It was windy and cold. But, we had been through worse, much worse, and nothing was going to deter me from reaching *Habibi*. It seemed like our only refuge from the cold – our shelter from the storm.

Finally, after about twenty-five minutes of walking, *Habibi* was within sight. I got a much needed boost of energy. My only fear was that it might be closed for the night.

We finally arrived. I hesitated for a moment, "Do not say anything, just sit down and I will order you something," I told him, before entering.

I heard some patrons speaking Arabic and I immediately grew uncomfortable with the environment. We picked a table in the corner and sat down, waiting for our waiter.

"Welcome to Habibi, what can I get you to start?" the waiter asked.

"Two glasses of water, an order of Falafel, and Hummus, please," I replied, keeping my head low.

"Falafel and Hummus, coming right up young men," he said, without writing down our order and heading back to the kitchen area.

He shouted, in Arabic, "Hummus and Falafel, yella, yella."

I scanned the diner and recognized that all, but one of the guests spoke, Arabic. This establishment resembled a café or restaurant in my hometown.

"Here you go gentleman. Your drinks, Hummus and Falafel," the waiter said, placing the plates in front of us.

"Thank you, sir," I nodded.

"My name is Malik, and I am the owner of *Habibi*.

What are your names?" he asked, as he pulled up a seat.

"I am Paul and this is my twin brother, Robert," I answered, apprehensively.

I wasn't sure why he asked, or sat down. But, as in most cases, the Middle Eastern culture is extremely welcoming and respectful to their guests, at home or at their place of business – just not at church.

"Happy you boys chose to come here. Are you from here? Or are you just visiting Frankfurt?" Malik asked, signaling his chef to prepare some special dish for our table.

"We just moved here from the United States, why are you asking?" I asked.

"Just curious, two young and smart boys walk into my restaurant that I have never seen before. Welcome to Germany boys," he replied, with a smile that oddly enough, made me feel at ease – like Uncle Al's.

"Let me take care of a table. I will be right back to sit and chat with you boys some more," Malik said, jumping up and catering to his other customers with the same enthusiasm and hospitality he'd shown us.

I was unsure what story I was going to tell Malik if he asked where we lived or anything about our parents. I'd be forced to make up something on the spot. The fear of being caught lying could set off a red flag, making Malik suspicious as to our intent and possibly call the authorities. But in the end, the only story worth telling would be the truth.

Malik grabbed a dish he ordered and brought it to our table, "Go ahead and enjoy. I made this for you boys."

"Amen," Robert shouted.

Malik nodded, "Yes, amen."

Robert did not hesitate. He grabbed his fork and began eating, again. As for me, I was too nervous to hold down any food, let alone enjoy it.

"So boys, how long are you and your family staying in Germany? Malik asked, sipping on his chai, "You staying here, in Frankfurt?"

I paused for a brief moment. I did not have the confidence to fool Malik. Maybe, a part of me did not want to deceive him. In a way, he reminded me of Uncle Al, with his hospitality and kind gestures.

It is true, what they say, *you don't know what you have until it's gone.* I was missing Uncle Al at the moment. His comforting and reassuring ways gave off a sense of security that made you feel safe when he was around.

"If I tell you something, in confidence, will you promise to keep it between us?" I asked Malik.

I leaned forward to whisper, watching his demeanor immediately change from relaxed and lighthearted, to a more stern and concerned one.

"Of course, my son, do not be afraid. You can tell me if there is anything bothering you," he replied, "What is it? Are you in trouble?"

"Well, I am not in trouble, as of yet. But, I am not supposed to be here, sir," I ambiguously answered.

I struggled to convince myself whether or not the truth was the best route.

"You left your home without asking your parents? That's what you did? Don't worry, I will call your father and explain that you are with me at the restaurant. And, I will drive you home when you are finished," he continued, leaning back with a relieved look on his face.

He smiled at us, but realized that my demeanor remained somber. He leaned forward, once again, "What is it? Tell me what the problem is and let me help you son. Are you in trouble with the law?"

"It is a bit of a long story. But I want you to know the truth, sir. I don't want to mislead you or deceive you in anyway. You have been too kind to us from the very beginning and the least I can do is repay you by telling you the truth. I just don't want to bother you or involve you in my troubles... I can handle it," I replied, my ego kicked in as my insecurities and fear of the unknown intensified.

Chapter 50

"Nonsense, you are in my restaurant, we are eating together and I will not sit by idle why you get yourself hurt. You are going to tell me what is bothering you or who is bothering you and I will handle it," he insisted, moving his chair next to mine, gesturing that it was okay to talk.

"You see, we are from Northern Iraq. About a year ago, my brothers and I were involved in an explosion. My youngest brother, Peter, was killed. Robert and I were obviously injured. Well, as you can probably tell, my brother is a bit more than slightly disabled," I said, fighting back tears at the memory of my youngest brother's death, compounded by the struggle and journey that I have been on for the last six or so months.

"Continue, tell me everything," Malik insisted, placing

his elbows on the table and hands under his chin.

He genuinely seemed concerned, a trait that most people from my culture possess, a Christian trait, I believed.

"We were flown to the United States by a gentleman named Al Davidson or Uncle Al as I know him to be now. He is the Chairman of an organization that aids and assists children in war torn countries," I continued.

Malik nodded and smiled, "Nice man."

"He really is," I nodded, "His organization picked up the tab on all our expenses, flight, housing, and medical bills. But, I soon realized that once their work was complete, their only option would be sending me back to where my nightmares began. A place that had no promise, no security, and no future – essentially, no longer my home," I added, losing the battle with my tears.

Malik tried to console me, "How did you end up in Germany?"

"Fate I guess. It was the layover before our final destination. This was my last chance at a new life. I was being sent back home, only to wake up waiting to die at the hands of some radical Muslim!" I replied, in anger and pain.

Malik's demeanor seemed to change, "I see now, you were a victim of a senseless act of violence at the hands of some radical Muslims."

I wiped my tears away, "Yes, and I do not want to go back to a place where a Muslim, who doesn't like me, because I was born a Christian, sets off a bomb that can possibly kill me, as it did Peter!" I snapped, allowing my anger to emerge from the horrifying memories that lolled violently still in my mind.

"I understand, do not worry my son, everything will be okay," he replied, nodding his head.

"That is what the Muslims back home told my family and me, and you can see what they have done. It is a lie and you can see for yourself! I hate all Muslims and I will never trust one again! You know how terrible they are, I'm sure you've dealt with their hate towards all the *infidels*. I want them to feel my pain. I want them to suffer as I have. There are no good Muslims... not one!" I exclaimed, pointing to my prosthetic limbs and finally to the sad state that was my brother.

"One second boys, I must make a phone call and I will return to finish dinner with you. You keep eating and if there is anything you need, just let me know," he said, standing up.

I wondered if Malik was contacting the authorities to turn us in for questioning and possibly arrest or even worse – deportation.

I quietly stood up and gestured to Robert, "Get up and follow me. I need to speak with you."

"I am not finished eating, Paul," he snapped, causing many patrons, including Malik, to turn their attention to us.

"Is everything okay, Paul?" Malik asked, covering the phone with his palm.

"Yes, everything is fine, sir. Thank you," I quickly replied.

I was furious and terrified at the same time; furious with Robert for raising his voice, and terrified at the probability that Malik was turning us in to the authorities.

"Robert, please get up. We must leave immediately," I said, with urgency, hidden in a veil of secrecy, so that only Robert would identify.

I treaded lightly fearing that another outburst would undoubtedly uncover my desperate desire to escape before capture.

I was too late, Malik was on his way back to our table and his expression was void of any visible emotion, at least to me.

"Boys, I have something to ask you?" Malik said, crossing his hands on the table and leaning forward, emphasizing the significance of the news.

"Do you know who I was on the phone with a moment ago?" he asked.

"No, I don't know, sir?" I asked, bracing myself for an answer that might alter my destiny.

"I was on the phone with my wife and I explained your situation. She is not only a teacher, but a crusader for human rights, and is extremely active at her church. She made it quite clear to me, and I must say, I agreed, that you two must stay with us until we find you a permanent home. What do you think about that, Paul, any objections?" he asked.

He was beaming with happiness at the chance to help in any way possible.

I was still a bit frightened and unsure if I could trust him. Although, he was a Christian man, as was Uncle Al. I was uneasy at the idea of staying at a stranger's home, but, at this point, what options did I have?

Could I have been this fortunate, after believing I was the most unlucky kid in the universe? First, I was blessed to meet, Charlie, then Uncle Al, and now Mr. Malik?

"Can I talk to Robert privately first, Malik, before I give you an answer?" I asked, concerned about his comfort and security.

"No problem. Take your time, talk amongst yourselves while I tend to some customers. I'll be back in about ten minutes or so. Come to a decision, please," Mr. Malik replied.

I pulled Robert to the side and sat him down. He seemed frustrated, probably over being repeatedly interrupted while eating, "Do you have any objections about staying at Mr. Malik's home for a few nights? Just until we find a permanent place to live," I asked.

"I just want to stay with you, Paul, just don't leave me behind," he replied, his innocence revealing the mind of a child.

"I would never leave you behind, never allow anything to happen to you, Robert, and you know that," I reassured him.

"Okay, let's head back to the table so you may finish eating and I will talk to Mr. Malik," I suggested, as we moved back to the table where Mr. Malik was awaiting our decision.

"So, boys, what have you decided?" Malik asked.

"We appreciate you offering us refuge from the cold, until we find a permanent home, Mr. Malik. I will call Uncle Al and inform him of our whereabouts and that we are in good hands," I replied, searching for any sign that this was some set-up or hidden agenda.

"Wonderful, I will let Anna know the good news! Anna is my wife, of course, and she is so excited to meet you boys. She is preparing a big dinner, so leave some room for more food. Although, I'll take some kabobs and chicken back home, Anna is making the best homemade Hummus you have ever tasted!" Malik exclaimed.

"Let me make sure my customers don't need anything. Then we will clean up and leave," Malik said, rushing off to cater to his customers.

Approximately an hour later, Malik began preparing to close down for the night. He and his help were busy cleaning up the dining area and kitchen.

"Can we help somehow, sir?" I asked, feeling guilty that we simply sat around, after being fed a wonderful meal and offered shelter, while he worked.

"Sure, thank you. Robert can help Ali clean up the kitchen, while you help me sweep and mop up the dining area. The quicker we get this done, the sooner we leave here and get home," he explained, giving me a broom and dustpan.

I nodded, "No problem."

"The mop and bucket are in the utility room in the back when you are finished sweeping, Paul," he added, cleaning up the tables and stacking the plates so that Ali and Robert finish their part.

The one thing that I truly appreciated about Malik was the fact that he never once made me feel uncomfortable about my handicap. He trusted me with cleaning up the dining room, like I was any able bodied teenager.

I was not going to forget the lessons I learned from Uncle Al. The honor in giving back was now paramount in my life. Malik now became Mr. Malik, out of respect. The same way I should have treated Uncle Al from that first awkward meeting at the airport.

Chapter 51

I felt guilty about being so kind and generous with Mr. Malik, almost like I was betraying Uncle Al. It was of no help that I continuously replayed the swearing incident in the Shriners lobby.

While mopping, I felt home sick. I don't think I had enough time to truly convey my feelings of gratitude and eternal appreciation. I don't believe Uncle Al knows just how much he meant to me.

I promised to contact Uncle Al at my first opportunity and I would. I wanted to hear his voice, and even more, I needed his blessings to continue.

"Okay boys, I think we're done here. Everyone wait outside while I turn on the alarm and lock the door," Mr. Malik instructed us.

I cautiously waited, scanning the perimeter for any

sign of trouble. I was undoubtedly still apprehensive at the entire arrangement. It just sounded too good to be true and, usually, if it sounds too good to be true – it probably is.

"Okay, let's go boys. Thank you, Ali, I will see you tomorrow morning, drive safely," Mr. Malik said, before heading towards his automobile.

We walked around the back of the restaurant to where Mr. Malik's car was, a late model sedan, not too new, not too old.

"Get in boys, Anna is waiting for us at home," Mr. Malik confirmed, as we jumped in, Robert in the back and I sat up front.

I paid close attention to our route and where exactly we were headed, just as a precautionary measure.

We drove for approximately twenty minutes, following main roads and twisting side roads as we finally reached our destination, a two story home that was located in a cul-de-sac of sorts.

"We're home, boys! Please grab the food, Robert, before you get out," Mr. Malik asked.

The kabob's smelled great, even before being cooked.

As we approached the house, a woman greeted Mr. Malik with a smile and enthusiasm generally associated with a reunion. It was just too surreal, too scripted, almost perfect, and picturesque.

"I am Anna, who is Paul and who is Robert?" She asked, leaning forward in Robert's face with a smile.

"He is Robert and I am Paul, ma'am. It is very nice to

meet you and thank you for welcoming us to your home on such short notice," I answered, trying to convey just how grateful we were for what they were doing.

Anna was a striking woman, in her mid-forties, I presumed, but did not look a day older than thirty! She was medium height, slender, with shoulder length blonde hair, big bright crystal clear blue eyes, and a light complexion.

The complete opposite of Mr. Malik, who stood approximately six feet tall, olive toned, with deep brown eyes, and short wavy hair. The one thing they did share was the warmth and hospitality that was second to none, a striking similarity to Uncle Al's generosity.

"Please boys, put your bags in the family room, for now, and rest while Malik and I prepare supper. I am sure you are both exhausted from the trip," Anna said, while Malik joined her in the kitchen where they began cooking.

"Thank you, ma'am, you and Mr. Malik are too kind," I replied, as Robert and I placed our bags near the family room.

We sat on the couch waiting for supper to be prepared, when I noticed the decorations that adorned the room were antiques and paintings. Based on that alone, Mr. Malik and Anna seemed like quite the travelers, or at the very least, a cultured couple.

"Can Robert and I help in anyway, ma'am?" I offered, feeling awkward that we just sat around.

"Don't be silly, you are our guests," Anna replied, looking back at us with a smile.

"You boys more than helped us at the restaurant and I never thanked you for that. So, thank you very much," he said, giving Anna a kiss on her cheek and sharing a smile with one another.

They seemed like the perfect couple, worldly, kind and in love. It all seemed surreal, as merely *twenty-four* hours earlier I was anxiously awaiting the result of my plan. To be afforded the comfort of a roof over our heads, food in our stomach, and hospitality from a wonderful *Christian* couple, seemed too good to be true.

"Turn on the television boys, there is a football game on tonight. Germany is at home against Italy in an exhibition game, it should be competitive. Do you follow it much?" Mr. Malik asked, glancing back to see our reaction.

"Yes, my brothers and I grew up playing football back home until those animals changed everything," I replied, looking at Robert.

"Great, you will enjoy today's game. We are obviously rooting for Germany, home team!" Anna declared, sticking her tongue out at Mr. Malik.

"I always liked Italy, but yes, tonight, we will root for the home team so that Anna does not hold back any special ingredient in her home made hummus!" Mr. Malik teased, while being poked by a spatula Anna was holding.

Watching them interact so affectionately towards each other made me miss my parents and the comfort of being with family. I longed to see my mother and father happy again. I didn't understand why *God* watched Muslims harm Christians.

"Dinner is ready boys!" Anna proclaimed, while Mr. Malik brought the food to the table.

I immediately stood up and gave them both a hand with the entrée they prepared.

We sat down together and enjoyed the meal as a family. Anna requested that Mr. Malik read a verse from the Holy Bible before we began eating. Anna had many questions for us, as did Mr. Malik. I, of course, answered them all, leaving Robert with the task of eating, which I may add, he handled perfectly.

Both Anna and Mr. Malik voiced their concerns over defecting to Germany, essentially, leaving them with very few, if any, options in handling the matter. Malik, however, did come up with a plan to get us identification, which would help us blend in and become a positive member of society while we were here.

After dinner, Mr. Malik and Anna spoke privately in the adjacent room and upon returning had asked for a moment to speak with us.

"We want you boys to stay with us, while you're in Germany. What do you think, Paul?" Anna asked.

Mr. Malik added, before I replied, "You cannot refuse this offer, Paul. We want you boys to be happy, after what those animals did to you both."

"I am just concerned about imposing on you, we're not your problem and you have already done too much, in my opinion," I answered, truthfully.

"Do not think like that. If you boys were too much, we would not extend the offer in the first place," Mr. Malik said, nodding.

"Where are your children?" Robert asked, catching both Anna and Mr. Malik off guard.

They smiled at one another, "We've been married for twelve years now. *God* wasn't ready to bless us with our own... until now," Anna replied, placing her hand on Robert's shoulder.

"Can I have a sister?" Robert asked, "I never had one before."

Mr. Malik and Anna both laughed, so did Robert. However, I was too embarrassed to join in.

"Yes, we'll work on it," Mr. Malik teased, winking at Anna.

"Fantastic! I will set up the guest room for tonight. Tomorrow you and Malik can purchase a second bed and squeeze in together until we figure out what to do," Anna quickly sealed the deal and changed the subject.

But I gave no resistance either, I was humbled and at the mercy of their hospitality.

In an odd way, I felt guilty for leaving Uncle Al behind after all he did for me. I laid there on the floor, struggling to sleep, while Robert had the bed. He had earned it, though.

Early the next morning, Robert and I entered the kitchen to find Mr. Malik and Anna preparing breakfast.

"Good morning, boys," they said, in harmony.

"Good morning, sir, good morning, ma'am," I replied,

as Robert sat down at the table, helping himself to some toast and butter.

"Paul, what do you think about you two boys helping me down at the restaurant to earn a little cash for your pocket, in case you would like to buy something for yourselves?" Mr. Malik offered, while preparing the food he would take to the restaurant with him.

"Robert will go with you, sir. I personally do not feel comfortable being around those kinds of people," I answered, my manners replaced with ugliness.

"Very well, Paul, I understand. Robert can come with me and help at the restaurant, while you sign up for a class at the local college. Maybe improve on some trade you are interested in. What do you think?" he asked, looking back to assure me that he was understanding and sympathetic to my feelings.

"Yes, I am extremely interested in advancing my education. I am very fond of computers and want to pursue a career that would utilize my talent," I replied, my anger subsided and felt a sense of relief washed over me.

"I think that would be best for Paul, build him a future that will allow him to stand on his own," she told Mr. Malik, before turning to me, "The local college would be perfect for you. Plus, I know a few professors who teach different courses and I can get you into their class with no problem," Anna said, smiling back at Mr. Malik and me.

"Great, it's settled then. Robert will help me out at the restaurant while Paul helps out at home when he is not in class," Mr. Malik confirmed, before giving Anna a kiss, grabbing the meats, the kabob skewers, his coat, and gesturing to Robert that it was time to leave.

To outsiders, the idea of allowing two strangers to move into their lives might have seemed odd. However, in my opinion, this was the standard of what being a good Christian couple meant to me; caring about your neighbor – no matter who they are.

Chapter 52

*T*he only thing that bothered me was the fact that Mr. Malik and Robert would be working with Muslims every day. That worried me quite a bit. My concern regarding the situation needed to be addressed. Although I feared causing a crack in our young relationship, it had to be done, soon... before it was too late.

I went online and searched through the classes being offered and found two classes that I was particularly interested in; computer programming, business management, and of course I would take a course in German.

I immediately registered for my classes. I was informed, online, that I had two weeks to reserve my seat by paying the tuition for the semester. I had the money to do so, just required a lift to school.

I rehearsed my speech before Mr. Malik and Robert got home. I was watching television in the family room, when I saw them pull up into the driveway.

"Anna, we're home, we brought some food as well. Paul, can you run to the car and help Robert bring in the left overs, please?" Mr. Malik asked, entering the house, grocery bags in hand.

"Yes sir, I also needed to speak with you tonight, if that's possible," I replied, heading to the car where I found Robert trying to pick up all the bags at once.

"Sure, let me get everything settled in and we can sit down and talk, Paul," he answered, stocking items away in the refrigerator and cabinets.

"How was it, Robert, did you have any trouble with those Muslims?" I whispered, trying to conceal my conversation from Anna and Mr. Malik.

"No, they were nice people, I like them," Robert replied, attempting to carry all the bags with one trip.

"Let me help with those, Robert, and what do you mean, *you liked them*?" I asked, growing irritated at the comment.

"The people at the restaurant were nice people, Paul. Very friendly with me and I liked them a lot. It reminds me of being home. I miss mom and dad, are we going to see them soon?" he asked, while his demeanor and temperament changed as if someone turned on a switch.

"Yes, soon we will see them both. Don't forget, Robert, those Muslims are the reason we are in this situation and suffered as we did," I reminded him, lowering my voice but emphasizing just how serious this was.

"They are not all bad people," Robert said, non-chalantly, finally conceding to picking up the few bags he held in his hand.

"Yes, they are, they are all the same and they only care about other Muslims. If they are called to fulfill the will of *Allah*, they would bomb the restaurant with you and Mr. Malik in it!" I snapped, turning my attention directly to Robert, hoping he would get my point.

"Do not trust them, just do your job, help Mr. Malik and come home until I figure this out. Do you understand me, Robert?" I asked, grabbing his arm turning him towards me.

"Yes, let go of me, you are hurting my arm, Paul," he shouted, pulling his arm from my grasp.

Robert was unusually strong, despite his mental condition, like he got physically stronger in order to make up what he lost, mentally.

I followed behind Robert into the house and towards the kitchen where Anna and Mr. Malik were preparing something to eat.

We placed the bags on the counter and began emptying them. I followed Robert's lead. This time, he seemed to know exactly what to do, and for the first time, I was not leading my *younger* brother.

"Paul, what did you want to talk to me about?" Mr. Malik asked, chopping up the vegetables for dinner.

"Sorry to interrupt, but, I was wondering if you boys wanted to attend church this Sunday?" Anna quickly jumped in, assuming our conversation would be lengthy.

"Yes, Robert and I would like that very much, Mrs. Anna, thank you very much," I replied, the tension and anxiety was now broken with that subtle offer, putting my mind back at ease.

"Great idea, Anna, I will come along as well," Mr. Malik added, they smiled at each other, sharing a moment that I had rarely witnessed my parents share.

"So, Paul, what was it you needed to speak to me about?" Mr. Malik asked, again.

I hesitated for a moment, aware of the loving atmosphere. I did not want to usher in a dark cloud of doubt and bitterness. Maybe I was overreacting, simply too cautious about Robert and Mr. Malik. Maybe they were safe and I just needed to keep my distance from Muslims.

"Actually, I needed a lift to the community college nearby. I registered for some classes. I must pay the fees and purchase the necessary text books. This must be completed as soon as possible. If you can, of course," I said.

I changed the story after realizing this was not the moment to bring up this subject, I did not want to be the person who spoils a nice evening with a hate filled speech, not tonight at least.

"Congratulations Paul! That is great news, I'd be happy to give you a lift. How about tomorrow, I don't open the restaurant on Saturdays until eleven anyways and we can be at your college at nine o'clock sharp," Mr. Malik replied, with an enthusiasm typically associated with the news of your son graduating college, not enrolling into one.

"Great, I am very excited for you, Paul. Tomorrow, you and Malik can head to the college and on Sunday, we will all attend church together. This is going to be a great weekend!" Anna added with the same enthusiasm Mr. Malik displayed as she smiled while helping prepare dinner.

As planned, Mr. Malik drove me to the college, but before I even paid for my classes, we were informed that I needed to provide a High School Diploma or the equivalent. Since I didn't one, I enrolled to take a G.E.D. class for the first semester and English, German, and Computer class, instead of the Business course, in the second semester.

After we completed what was required of me, Mr. Malik and I spent the rest of the early afternoon at a café, where we talked about the future and what it had in store for us all.

I spent the remainder of the evening in my room with Robert, browsing the internet on college courses and more importantly, updates on my Uncle Al. I set the alarm to wake me up early to attend church. I was well-aware of the sacrifices Uncle Al made to mend my heart towards the church and my *God* and I wouldn't let him down.

My alarm clock went off at eight O'clock, sharp. I jumped up and tapped Robert with my foot in passing towards the bathroom to shower. By the time I left the bathroom, Robert was dressed and downstairs having breakfast with Mr. Malik and Anna.

I skipped breakfast knowing that eating prior to taking your communion was not acceptable in my culture. Quite honestly, I was shocked to see Mr. Malik and Anna ignoring that universal fact as well, but I didn't judge. It was not too long ago that a certain someone cursed *God* himself and if it was not for Uncle Al, might still be doing so to this very day.

"Good morning, Paul, you look very nice this," Anna said, giving me a hug.

"Good morning, Paul, are you hungry?" Mr. Malik asked, eating with Robert.

"I am going to eat after service, if that is alright," I replied, hoping not offend them by refusing breakfast.

"No problem, we're actually ready to leave now. Robert, you ready?" Mr. Malik asked, as he and Anna stood up from the kitchen table.

"Yes, I am ready now," Robert answered, while still eating as he stood up, finishing his plate and placing it in the sink.

We followed out, one after the other. We hopped into the car and headed to church. I wasn't sure what to expect at a German church, compared to my Orthodox one, as long as they were Christian.

We drove for fifteen minutes in silence, brief interludes between topics with Anna and Mr. Malik, all the while, Robert and I sat quietly in the back. We arrived at the Cathedral and pulled into an extremely large parking lot located in the back of the church.

The parking lot was filled to capacity. I had never seen this many cars parked in front of any building in my life. I grew anxious. I realized the sheer magnitude of people, alone, would pose a danger to my true identity. Or at the very least, force me to adopt an alias that wasn't my own – permanently.

Chapter 53

"Good morning, Anna, very nice to see Malik with you today," a passerby said.

"Thank you and a good morning to you as well, ma'am," Anna replied, smiling at Mr. Malik and holding hands.

"Very nice to have you both with us on this blessed Sunday morning and just who are these two fine young lads, Anna," a man asked who was either the priest or the pastor of the church.

"Reverend, these two lovely boys are Paul and Robert; they are Malik's nephews who are staying with us for a while. Boys, this is reverend Conrad, he is the Pastor at our church here," Anna said, introducing us as family.

"Good morning, Reverend, very honored to meet you," I said, accepting his hand in greeting with my left, as I was still uncomfortable extending my prosthetic. Typically, our Priests would extend their hand so the people kiss the Holy Ring. But in this case, Reverend Conrad simply shook our hands as if there was no difference between himself and his congregation.

"I'm very happy to see you all here, Malik, you especially. Boys, glad to meet you and I hope you enjoy my sermon today. I wish you were here last week, Anna had some great ideas and we could have definitely used your opinions," Reverend Conrad said, before hurrying off to greet other members of his congregation.

"Thank you, reverend," Mr. Malik added, smiling at Anna as we followed him to the pews, sitting at the back of the church.

It was not strange to me that many church members were stealing peaks at Mr. Malik and Anna, since they had shown up with two teenage boys. But it seemed a bit more than just that, something I could not put my finger on quite yet. Besides the fact that Robert and I were disabled, there was something more. I was curious about it now and wanted to find the answer. In time, all things unveil themselves naturally.

On my way to receive my communion, I was conscious of saying a special prayer for Uncle Al, back in the United States and I hoped he would sense it.

We spent the evening, after church, at home together playing board games and having a nice time. It was the first feeling of home I've had since this tragedy. I couldn't help but stand amazed at how life can take you on a roller coaster ride, from low points to the high ones, as it does, so effortlessly.

The next few months of my life went on with the same routine, attending my classes while Robert had become an almost permanent employee of Habibi. The living situation subject become a non-issue and was rarely, if ever, spoken about. The chemistry between us had become natural, like we were meant to come together all along.

Mr. Malik would hint at the idea that I try to make contact with my family, at least to let them know that we were safe, if not, where we were. Enough time had passed where any type of contact back home was as safe now, as it would ever be in the future.

The summer had now come and gone, making way for the crisp autumn wind that introduces the bitter cold winter. One thing I missed dearly was the Christmas gatherings my family had back home. The cold wasn't too harsh but just enough to give you that holiday spirit.

The four of us spent the Christmas holiday together at home. Mr. Malik had found a beautiful Christmas tree for Anna that we helped pick out and decorate. We ushered in the New Year together and for the first time, in a while, I felt an empty sadness rest gently in my stomach, a feeling of disconnection and abandonment – a loss of identity.

My mind wandered back to the United States, specifically Los Angeles, where Uncle Al lived. I wondered if he thought about us anymore. Did he miss us? I surely missed him and his presence. He was truly a wonderful human being.

I promised myself that once I graduated, I would fly to the United States and surprise him with my success. Show him the fruits of his labor, the product of his dedication, and goodwill. He saved my life and I wanted him to be proud of me.

I focused on my grades and excelled in each of my classes. I was determined to succeed. I told myself, I have come this far and nothing was going to deter me from achieving my goals.

Until one fateful day after class in the college cafeteria, I happen to bump into a fellow student who would alter my life.

"Pardon me, I didn't see you there," I said, my eyes were glued to this figure that stood before me.

"Not to worry, you must be hungry. Hi, I'm Joanna, what is your name?" she asked, staring at me with her big green eyes and a smile that light up a dark and starless sky.

I hesitated, inspecting her entirely, from the top of her head to the tips of her toes that were protruding from her sandals, "Hi, my name is Paul. I have never seen you here before, just recently registered?" I asked, as cool as Elvis Presley.

"I registered last semester, taking a course in psychology and child development. I want to become a child counselor when I am done with school," Joanna replied, keeping that glowing smile available for me to enjoy.

"That is beautiful, I think that is great," I answered, not knowing what else to say but knowing that silence would be better served until I identified the feeling that resided in my heart.

"I am going to be late for class, but I would like to exchange numbers if you don't mind. Stay in contact, who knows, I might need your help with some school project," Joanna said, writing down her number, while I remained dumbfounded by her beauty.

"You can call me later tonight, Paul, if you like me, of course," she giggled, walking away.

"I will call you tonight," I replied, as quickly as possible, abandoning the cool role with each step that separated us now.

"You promise?" she asked.

"Yes, I promise. I will call you tonight," I crooned, stuck in a trance, mind and body awakened. Feelings that lay dormant since my affair with the *Goddess of Love*.

I admired and adored the relationship that Mr. Malik and Anna shared. I had now, my very own, Anna. I was getting a bit ahead of myself and I knew it. But... for a brief moment, I dared to dream again.

The next weeks turned into months. Joanna and I became inseparable. We spent hours upon hours chatting. And every minute, we could, together. I can honestly say that my life was now normal. With each drop of happiness and every ounce of confidence that grew within me, I could not help but to think about Uncle Al. I told Joanna all about him and my plans to visit him again. She seemed fascinated with as well and also desired to meet this wonderful hero of mine.

Mr. Malik, Anna, and even Robert loved Joanna and supported us in every way imaginable. In Mr. Malik, I had found a role model, a Christian man I can imitate when dealing with a loved one. My father wasn't the romantic type, nor was he truly gentle or supporting of my mother. But then again, what Middle Eastern man I knew growing up was?

I attempted to place the final piece of the puzzle the night Joana and I spent together at church. I was a bit apprehensive, even anxious about Easter, this time around, more than before, in part because I was happy once again. I couldn't help revisiting the time Ishtar and I spent together, and that fateful Easter day when my anguish began.

I couldn't help but think the worst while sitting in church with Mr. Malik, Anna, Robert and Joanna. My thoughts ran amok, I imagined horrific scenario's that seemed so real I could touch them. A battle for my soul was rattling my spirit. The winner would be the one I'd serve.

Chapter 54

"Are you okay, Paul?" Joanna asked, noticing my cold hand and awkward disposition.

"Yes, I am fine, just a lot on my mind," I replied, dreading the notion of explaining my nightmares.

I was terrified of leaving church and secretly hoped the sermon never ended. Just thinking about opening those doors, and hearing silence, once again, shook me to my bone. I lost all control over my mind. I excused myself to go wash my face, take a deep breath, and compose myself.

The sermon ended, and while many of the congregation gathered around, wishing each other a Happy Easter, I was fixated on what lie in the darkness waiting, outside those doors. An overwhelming feeling of terror was now brewing in my stomach, slowly cueing that I may vomit.

As the final handshakes and well wishes were received, the four of us head towards the exit. The next few steps felt like I was walking in sand. Mr. Malik opened the door with Anna and Robert following. Joanna waited behind to hold the door open for me. I crossed the threshold leading me outside and anticipated the worst.

We passed the steps in front of the church and reached the sidewalk, where I felt a bit better. We entered the car and drove away when I finally accepted that my life was firmly back on track.

"That was fun, thank you," I said.

We all shared a smile and enjoyed the rest of our day.

Months turned to years, and I finally proposed to Joanna who accepted. The next year, we tied the knot in a small ceremony, with just a few friends and family in attendance. I had spoken to my parents but never able to see them, nor were they able to be present at my wedding. I felt guilty about their inability to celebrate with their son.

Although my life had more than its fair share of tragedy, it also contained brief flashes of bliss. Joanna and I welcomed our first child to our family, Peter, named after my late brother. We added a middle name as well, Al. Peter Al in honor of the two people I'd never forget.

I sometimes sat and watched Peter run around being a little boy without a care in the world. He was removed from the realities of life, distant in the grim tragedies that time offered.

The more I watched Peter grow, the more I ignored any disabilities I had. I no longer was the most important person in my world. My family was now my hands, my legs, my strength, and my foundation.

Over the years I have endured some tragedy in my life. The death of my father was followed quickly by the death of my mother a mere ten months later was a devastating shock to me, and Robert.

The death of my parents made me worried about Uncle Al and brought up a major concern of mine. Every day that passed was one day closer to being too late. I didn't want to delay this visit any longer.

"I'm ready to go visit Uncle Al," I told Joanna.

She smiled and hugged me, "I'm happy for you."

We decided that it would be a surprise, since he loved pulling pranks on people; we thought we should return the favor. I must admit, I was extremely nervous about my trip. It had been more than twenty years since I last seen Uncle Al.

Although, over the years, I kept in touch with him via email and sometimes on the phone, we had not spoken in almost two years. But, I had no doubt that sense of humor and generous heart would always remain a constant trait, a virtue that never betrayed him.

We arranged my Visa for a six month visit, as a German citizen. I informed Mr. Malik and Anna about our surprise trip to the states to see Uncle Al and both of them couldn't have been more supportive and happy for me.

"Hi, Robert," I said, patting my twin brother on his back.

"How are you, Paul," he replied.

"I'm good. I see you're doing well yourself. Listen, you know I'm heading to the states to see Uncle Al, are you interested in coming along?" I asked.

He shook his head, "No, not, really. Just tell him I said thank you. He'll know what I mean."

I smiled, "He'll know what you mean?"

He nodded, "Yup."

I didn't say a word. I just admired my brother for a minute.

"I love you, brother. I'll see you when I get back," I said, kissing his head.

We finally arrived in the United States, approximately twenty-three years from the time a young teenage boy boarded a plane which was headed for the Middle East, but the final destination remained unknown.

I was excited to surprise Uncle Al and thrilled to see him. I had confirmed that his home address remained as it did more than two decades ago when I was a visitor, unaware that my relationship with this loving man would endure a lifetime.

We arrived a bit late in the states and feared that visiting him this late would arouse suspicion. Joanna and I agreed to rent a room at a nearby hotel, deciding that we'd surprise him at his office with an invitation to breakfast or brunch.

I struggled to sleep all night, I was so anxious to

finally reunite with my Uncle Al. I jumped out of bed at approximately eight in the morning and got dressed as Joanna showered. We were on the road a quarter past ten as we made our way down Ventura Boulevard and towards his office. We pulled around the side and into the parking garage. One thing I noticed, I was calm and collected.

We quickly walked to the front door and I paused to take a deep breath.

Joanna gave me a reassuring smile, "He's waited twenty years. You shouldn't make him wait any longer."

We walked up to the counter where a young lady greeted us, "Can I help you?"

"Yes, I am here to see Al Davidson, please," I asked, trying to conceal my voice, preserving the surprise.

"Who should I say is here to see him," she asked.

"I would like for my identity to remain a secret, please. If you can just tell Mr. Davidson to come out for a second, he would be most surprised and happy that you did," I assured her.

"Okay, give me one second. Please take a seat and I will be back in a moment," she said, walking towards Uncle Al's office door.

I looked around to find some pictures of new faces and only one remaining picture of Uncle Al himself – an old picture at that. That was my Uncle Al, always putting others ahead of himself. Giving was better than receiving was always his motto and, in every scenario, he practiced what he preached.

After a few minutes of waiting, a gentleman approached us. He was dressed in a nice charcoal suit and wore a ponytail. I recognized him from a picture on the wall in the foyer.

"Good morning, ma'am and good morning, sir. How can I help you?" the ponytailed man asked. "Please, sit."

"Yes, I wanted this to be a secret. My name is Paul, I was a patient of Uncle Al's more than two decades ago and I wanted to surprise him. I have not seen Uncle Al since I left the United States when I was just a teenager," I explained, concerned that I might have caught him while he's out of town.

There was a brief pause. The ponytailed man finally looked at me with an expression that needed no translation, "I'm sorry to inform you, but, Al passed away a year ago. I am so sorry to break the news," the ponytailed man said, who seemed to share my sorrow.

Joanna sat quietly, just holding me. I was numb and speechless. My mind wandered in an ocean of desolation. I felt pain in my heart. I hurt, but only imagined the memories we shared.

"I am sorry, Paul. I do remember your story though and if it's any consolation, Al spoke about you with such love and pride. He always referred to you as his son and you constantly remained in his thoughts," he added, also fighting back tears as he seemed to be mourning.

"Who was Uncle Al to you, if you don't mind me asking?" my curiosity grew regarding this man's relationship with Uncle Al.

The ponytailed man seemed about my age, but judging by his looks, father time had been kind to him.

"Al Davidson was my mentor, my teacher. I am the man I am today because of him, and for that, I will always remain in mourning. I will honor him, his life, and carry the torch of his legacy and goodwill, which he devoted his entire life to," he continued, losing a tough fought battle with his tears, who now marched triumphantly down his face.

We all sat in silence, each reminiscing about their memories. He inspired me to always believe, never give up on hope, and always trust in *God*. My life was my bond with him.

We stood up and shared our farewells. The ponytailed man walked away and disappeared behind the walls.

We walked out of the office and sat in the car. We just sat an absorbed it all in. I stared out to the street and the people walking around me. I couldn't help but think that these folks have no idea that a saint walked amongst us.

Joanna and I did not stay another day in the City of Angels. We boarded a plane that night and flew to Hawaii instead. I knew this was my last goodbye to the United States – my final curtain call.

Chapter 55

The first few nights in Hawaii were a bit blue for me, a bitter sweet memory.

I wondered if I'd apologized enough to Uncle Al for my selfish behaviors all those years ago. I just hoped he knew how much I appreciated everything he, the Shiners Hospital, and the Ronald McDonald House did for my family.

We planned to visit the Shriners Hospital with Uncle Al, but, I couldn't bear standing inside a palace where the person I believed to be a king was dead.

I can hear Uncle Al's voice; *enjoy your life, live on the square, be good to your fellow man, of honorable service to your community, and loyal to your country.*

We stayed in Hawaii for two weeks before I received a

phone call from Anna, "Paul, Malik is not feeling well. I've admitted him to the hospital here in Frankfurt, near the home."

"Is he okay?" I asked.

"Yes, just please get home as soon as you can," she replied, though her voice told another story altogether.

"We'll be on the next flight home. Is Robert okay?" I asked.

"Yes, he is doing fine. A bit confused, but okay for the most part," she said.

I was extremely anxious to get home. We rushed back to our hotel room, packed our bags, and caught the first available flight back to Germany. I was not a big drinker, but without some type of suppressant, I would not reach Germany with my sanity.

The negative feelings overwhelmed me with inconceivable thoughts, each claiming residency in my mind; arranging their beliefs like old furniture.

We arrived in Frankfurt and quickly retrieved our bags, almost leaving one behind in the panic. I checked my voice mail to verify what hospital Mr. Malik was admitted in. We hailed a cab and immediately headed in that direction. As we reached the hospital, Joanna paid the cab fare and I rushed through the emergency doors and to the front counter.

"Malik Yousif, what room can I find him in please?" I asked the lady at the information desk.

"He is in room 102 and is currently with doctors," she replied, handing Joana and me name tags, and pointing us in the right direction.

I grabbed Joanna's hand and rushed down the corridor towards his room. I was afraid of losing Mr. Malik. I just couldn't handle any more tragedy. We reached the waiting room to find Anna sitting with her coffee, reading the paper.

"Anna, is Mr. Malik okay?" I asked, as she jumped out of her seat and we embraced.

Robert was sitting in the room as well, Joanna sat and spoke to him as Anna and I talked.

"He will be fine, Paul, do not worry. He just had a minor heart attack but the doctors say he'll be okay," Anna informed me, her eyes were red and swollen.

"When can I see him?" I asked.

I knew my faith was being tested by *God*. I had endured the loss of Uncle Al, both my parents. I couldn't handle losing my guardian as well. I needed to see Mr. Malik alive and well for me to relax. Nothing short of that would pacify me now.

I continued towards Mr. Malik's room. I reached room 102 and I hesitated. I was afraid of seeing the man I spent the last twenty plus years with in any type of pain. The thought of losing Mr. Malik devastated me.

I cautiously entered Mr. Malik's room. His door was slightly open, enough for me to peak in. To my surprise, he was not in bed, it was empty and I slowly walked in looking for him. I was about to call out for him when I witnessed something that shook me to my core.

I fell back and took a deep breath. I tried to maintain

my composure but my heart raced. My body weakened by the betrayal set by my eyes.

I could not believe what I saw, there must have been some type of mistake... this was not Mr. Malik's room.

I walked backwards a few steps and glanced at the room number and confirmed.

Anna nodded, "Is he okay?"

But it couldn't be. It just cannot be the Mr. Malik I spent the last twenty plus years with – this was not the same man.

I took some more time to regain my composure and quietly entered the room once again. I hoped my eyes had deceived me. But there was Mr. Malik, on the floor praying. Although I could not decipher the words, I heard him reciting a verse in Arabic.

I shook my head in disbelief. My mind couldn't fathom what it was seeing. However, my heart had already initiated the mourning process.

I watched in horror while the man who became like a father to Robert and me continue this ritual. A million thoughts ran through my mind, when did this happen? There must be a good explanation for all this. Yet, I had to hear it from his mouth.

Mr. Malik stopped praying and stood up, when I quickly left the room without giving away my presence. I was not ready to confront him, not ready to hear the answers to the questions that eroded my soul. I was terrified of the answers, horrified by the possibilities. For the first time in recent memory, I feared the only thing constant in my life... the truth.

I gave myself a few more minutes, summoning the courage, before having to face the truth. I was convinced there was a rational explanation, an answer that eluded me in my panic. I was positive about that, just something I didn't understand, his prayer ritual was different, and I wasn't an expert anyway.

I began heading back to the waiting room and sit with the rest of the family. Halfway down the hall I stopped, I could not just leave without knowing.

I returned to the room to find Mr. Malik sitting on his bed now watching the television. I took one final deep breath and entered the room.

"I got here as soon as I heard, are you okay, Mr. Malik?" I asked, maintaining a calm voice.

We embraced, while the fear of losing my step-father had been now mixed with the confusion of what I saw a few moments earlier.

"I will be fine, Paul, do not be worried. I am a tough old man and I have too much to life ahead of me," he replied, brandishing the smile that always comforted me in my time of despair.

"I am sorry about your Uncle Al. Anna told me that you left a voice mail and sounded heartbroken. Take comfort in knowing that you and he shared a bond that will go beyond the borders of this life and carry across into the next one," Mr. Malik continued, placing his hand on my shoulder.

"I am just sad that I wasn't able to say goodbye to him.

I didn't tell him just how grateful I was for all that he did. That I owe him for the life I live today, the people I call family. I just wanted him to know that I never stopped thinking about him, I moved away, but never moved on," I confessed.

"He knew, Paul, he was aware of just how special what you shared was," Mr. Malik added, as we embraced once again sharing a moment of relief and understanding.

We sat still for a time, just taking it all in. I was too afraid to open the conversation, fearing what road it might take us on. I worried about steering our relationship to parts unknown, an imaginary line of no return. I dreaded the notion that it might fracture, or even worse... break our special kinship.

"What is wrong, Paul, something is bothering you my, son," he asked, turning down the volume of the television set.

"Nothing, Mr. Malik, everything is fine as long as you are," I replied, avoiding eye contact with him.

"Paul, I know you well enough to recognize when something is bothering you. Do not lie to me, you never have, and please do not start now. What is really troubling you? Please tell me," Mr. Malik continued.

I feared putting any unnecessary stress on him, given his condition. I stared at the television but my thoughts were exclusively with him.

"I am waiting. Paul, you are well aware that you can speak to me about anything, my son," he reminded me.

"I don't know how to say this. I'm not even sure if

there is *anything* to say," I replied, avoiding the subject, which was, at least for me, taboo.

"Just say it, whatever it is. Do not keep it bottled up inside you," he encouraged me.

"When I first arrived to see you, I walked in and found you kneeling. I don't know what to think, I just saw you on the floor... praying. But that's not how Christians pray," I admitted, my confusion grew larger after I heard my question aloud.

There was a long pause. I finally mustered up the courage to look Mr. Malik in the eyes, as he now failed to return the favor. I was terrified of what he might say next. A terribly chilling feeling saturated the walls around us.

"Paul, when you first arrived in my life, you were scared and vulnerable. You had anger within you towards all Muslims. You seemed blinded by pure hate. You possessed a prejudice opinion that blanketed the entire religion over the actions of a small group of mentally disturbed idiots," Mr. Malik revealed, now looking at me with an unwavering confidence that his gospel would be accepted.

"If your question is, 'am I a Muslim?' Yes, Paul, I am and have been a practicing Muslim all my life. Does that change who I am? Does that erase all the years we have spent together as a family? Does that void the fact that Anna and I took you and Robert in as our own without question or concern about your beliefs or ours? I can tell you, unequivocally, that it shouldn't, my son," Mr. Malik added.

As I stared at the floor in shock at the confession

before me, uncertain if I felt anger and betrayal or was it guilt and shame. Anger and betrayal at the fact that Mr. Malik and Anna hid the truth from us for all these years or shame and guilt that my ignorance and hate had forced Malik, whom I loved and consider my father, to hide his true identity and basically – live a lie.

"So Anna is a Muslim as well?" I asked, unsure of what was true anymore.

"No, Anna is a Christian and a good one at that," Malik replied, as a matter of fact.

I remained silent, absorbing all of the information I had received. I hoped to place everything I had just learned into perspective and not just mine. The more I allowed the moment to wane, the less dramatic it all became.

The fact that Mr. Malik was a Muslim became irrelevant to me. I spent all of these years believing he was a noble and honorable Christian man only to find out that all this time, he had been a noble and honorable Muslim man.

"Paul, my son, you and Joanna are raising a family of your own. Ask yourself; what type of man do you want Peter Al to be? What kind of example are you going to be for your children?" Mr. Malik added, as the point he conveyed became clearer with every word.

"Do you love me, Paul? Do you think I am a good man? Have I been good to you?" he continued, holding my hand.

I looked at him and recalled all the times Robert and I were sick, afraid, or just in need of some objective advice.

The one constant figure in those most trying times was Mr. Malik, a good man who also happened to be a Muslim.

"Yes, I do, Mr. Malik, and yes, you have been more than good to Robert and me," I answered, I finally managing a smile.

I needed Mr. Malik to know that my respect and love for him could not be changed, for any reason, whatsoever. Yet, there were still some questions that I needed answered.

"But you attended church, celebrated Christmas, and Easter. We decorated the Christmas tree together and opened gifts. You recited *our father* for years at the dinner table. So that was all an act?" I asked, now more curious as to how he managed to pretend to be someone he was not, for so long.

"No, I was not pretending, Paul, and I meant every word of *our father*. I enjoyed every moment I spent with all of you at church. There is no difference between a sincere Christian, Muslim, or Jewish person. To me, if you are honest and mature in your faith, it will resonate in your actions. Keep in mind, the essence of the Abrahamic Religions is that *God is love and love is blind*," Mr. Malik answered.

Tears rolled down my eyes and rested gently on his pillow.

I immediately felt a sense of relief. The years of pressure had been lifted off my shoulders. I lived under the cloud of hate for all of my adult life. All that anger, that hostility that clawed at my soul and eroded the very fabric of my being was now slowly, but surely... a distant memory.

We silently sat together. Communication was unnecessary in the *now*. Our understanding was beyond words and the message was clear; *true love is blind*. We laughed and reminisced about times Mr. Malik was forced to conceal his faith just to avoid the topic. He continued telling one story after the next, while I couldn't help but think; just how great of a man he truly has been.

I've learned that it doesn't matter who put your faith in. The most important virtue is that you have faith, believe in mankind, goodwill, and in spreading the truth that *God is love and love is blind*.

So, you see, the story of my life has been both unique and rewarding to say the least. But, not entirely due to the fact that I was a Christian born in an Islamic country. But more than that, I was able to live a life where I realized that as your faith matures and you are honest to yourself, you'll discover there is no difference between a Christian, Jew, or Muslim.

My journey has *indeed* consisted of lessons that have taught me to be a patient, understanding, and compassionate man. Leading me to an epiphany, best summed up by a prayer; *you must help your brother along the way, no matter where he starts, for the same God that made you, made him too, these men with noble hearts.*

Amen.

ACKNOWLEDGEMENTS

This story is dedicated to all those kids around the world inflicted by famine, disease, and war.

To my precious mother, you showered me with unconditional love and taught me to treat others the same. I've learned that no matter how many mountains I conquer, without love, I have nothing at all.

To my Mason Brethren around the world, regardless of where you are dispersed, I am with you in spirit.

Herbert Oliver Christopher, Past Master of Masonic Lodge; a father figure to me, I thank you for nominating and presenting me with the Hiram Award. Words cannot express how honored and humbled I was to be recognized by such noble individuals.

Milton J. Nenney, my mentor and noble Brother Mason. You nurtured me with love and patience. Rest in peace, my brother, until we meet again.

Willard Vausbinder and David Haldeman, Past Potentates, respectively, thank you for nominating and trusting me to the Board of Governors of Shriners Hospitals for Children – Los Angeles, where I humbly served for ten years.

Shriners Hospitals for Children, greatest philanthropic organization in the world, thank you for teaching me that the true meaning of charity is imbedded in service to mankind.

To the Assyrian Church of the East and his Holiness, Mar Dinkha, your Grace blesses us all.

To Father George Bet Rasho, I am humbled by your message of love, faith, and hope. You have unconditionally supported our mission and I am eternally grateful.

To my Assyrian brothers and sisters, words cannot express how proud I am of our heritage. An incumbent duty that comes with this history is that we remain united, continue to promote peace, and love as our Lord and Savior Jesus Christ bestowed upon the world.

And finally, to my most proudest achievement, my family... the interpretation of being lucky can differ from one individual to another, yet for me it is simple, to have a family full of love.

To my beautiful partner in life, my wife, Maureen, you remain my happiness and source of strength. I cannot imagine my life without you. I love you, always.

Anita, you have been an angel to me from the second you were born. Your love for life and smile brightens my day. I am as proud as a father can be. I love you, unconditionally.

A father's joy is a son that exceeds his own standards. Allen, I proudly declare that you have done so and much more. Your integrity, honesty, and compassion inspire me to keep raising my principles as well. I will always support you and be there when you need me, my son.

George G. Edwards, about 6,763 years ago, in the ancient land of Mesopotamia, we stood side by side as comrades. Finally, we reunited in September of 2012, only this time as family – father and son.

~ Albert Davidoo

To my beloved mentor, Rabi Albert Davidoo, we are kindred spirits – thousands of years old. I will proudly carry the torch of your legacy for the rest of my days. Here's to a happy and lifelong kinship, cheers!

I would like to thank my brilliant editor, Cliff Carle, whom I cannot hide for myself; so I'll share with the world.

Special thanks to two wonderfully gifted artists:

Renee Barratt, your eye for the perfect cover is impeccable.

Elaine Lanmon, thank you for an absolutely wonderful job done.

Rosebud, you are my foundation – I love you.

Finally, fellow citizens of the world... let there be love!

~ George G. Edwards

www.ingramcontent.com/pod-product-compliance
Lightning Source LLC
Chambersburg PA
CBHW030033180626
46810CB00001B/355